W

T. MILBURN

THE WRATH OF IRON EYES

The notorious but disfigured bounty hunter Iron Eyes merely hunted men for the price of their head and then killed them without compunction. But when he encounters the beautiful daughter of a banker, he finds a woman who does not turn away from his horrific appearance. Riding after yet another outlaw, Iron Eyes is attacked and wounded by Indians. He then discovers that Mexican bandits have kidnapped the banker's daughter and so, barely alive, he uses his unique hunting skills to track the villains . . .

RORY BLACK

THE WRATH OF IRON EYES

Complete and Unabridged

LINFORD
Leicester

First published in Great Britain in 2003 by
Robert Hale Limited
London

First Linford Edition
published 2004
by arrangement with
Robert Hale Limited
London

British Library CIP Data

Black, Rory
    The wrath of Iron Eyes.—Large print ed.—
Linford western library
    1. Western stories
    2. Large type books
    I. Title
    823.9'14 [F]

ISBN 1–84395–312–9

ULV 18 . 5 . 04
LO   24. 6 . 04

Published by
F. A. Thorpe (Publishing)
Anstey, Leicestershire

Set by Words & Graphics Ltd.
Anstey, Leicestershire
Printed and bound in Great Britain by
T. J. International Ltd., Padstow, Cornwall

This book is printed on acid-free paper

Dedicated with thanks
to the world's finest comic book artist,
my friend Bill Black

1

The cruel storm had started just before sundown. By the time darkness had overwhelmed the bounty hunter, he was drenched to the bone. The lightning flashes above the desolate range gave the grim rider brief glimpses of his prey. But never long enough or close enough for Iron Eyes to pick him off.

It was like trying to catch the lightning itself, but Iron Eyes refused to quit. He had invested too much time to even consider stopping his relentless pursuit.

Every few minutes the narrow, cold-steel eyes spotted the fleeing rider as forked lightning splintered from the sky and found something on the ground to strike. Rain poured down mercilessly, stinging the hide of the bedraggled pony and its determined master who refused to give up.

It felt to Iron Eyes that he had incurred the wrath of the very elements themselves as he drove the spent pony on and on knowing the man he was hunting had a far superior animal beneath his saddle. But this did not stop his attempt to gain ground on the horse-thief he had been tracking.

Then Iron Eyes felt his mount stumble and knew that if he were to catch up with the man he was chasing, he had to allow the pony to rest for a few minutes. Iron Eyes drew in his reins and sat astride the exhausted animal, watching the black horizon for clues to where his prey had gone. For more than five minutes the bounty hunter waited for another flash of lightning to illuminate the scene. Then it was as if the heavens had declared war on the very earth beneath it. Bolts of white lightning carved twisted routes down out of the clouds above him. Cactus and joshua trees took the full impact of the electrical strikes, exploding into flames all around the mounted rider until the ceaseless rain extinguished them.

Suddenly the pony jolted in terror as Iron Eyes gripped his reins firmly in his bony hands and fought to maintain control of the skittish animal.

Only when the pony collapsed beneath him and he hit the ground did Iron Eyes hear the sound of the rifle shots above the deafening roar of the thunderclaps.

He rolled away from the horse and drew both his pistols from his belt. As light flashed across the prairie again he saw his quarry firing directly at him from atop a ridge. Bullets flashed over the dead horse, narrowly missing the bounty hunter. Iron Eyes blasted both his Navy Colts at the horse-thief but his shots were short of range.

The horseman let loose again.

The wet ground splashed all around Iron Eyes as the bullets of the horse-thief's Winchester tried to kill his hunter as neatly as it had finished off the pony.

Iron Eyes threw himself down next to the dead animal and tried desperately to pull his own rifle from its scabbard beneath the saddle. It was no use, the carbine was trapped under the full weight of the stricken horse.

Another volley of lead hit the carcass of the pony. Iron Eyes kept down behind its bulk and gritted his teeth. He knew that unless the rider came within range of his trusty pistols, there was no way he could kill the outlaw.

But although Ben Drake was a skilled horse-thief and a reasonable shot, he was also not stupid. There was no way he was going to ride into the range of the Navy Colts.

As another flash of lightning lit up the scene, Iron Eyes watched the rider turning his dapple-grey mount around and then ride off into the darkness.

Iron Eyes rose to his feet and stared through the driving rain at where he had last seen the elusive Ben Drake. Without a second's hesitation, the long-legged man unbuckled his saddlebags from the dead pony, tossed them over his shoulder and started to walk after the outlaw.

He had no idea how far it was to the next town, but he knew that Drake would go there and feel confident enough to stay, knowing that the one man who had dogged his trail for so many days was on foot out on the range.

After only a few minutes of walking through the pouring rain, Iron Eyes started to increase his pace until he was no longer merely walking.

He was running.

As the sky mocked his every stride, Iron Eyes continued running into the unknown. He knew that it was only a matter of time before he would catch up with the man he was hunting and claim the reward.

Horse-thieves were wanted dead or alive and that suited Iron Eyes just fine.

Ben Drake was living on borrowed time.

Ben Drake had a bounty on his head. A bounty that Iron Eyes had already determined would be his.

2

Lightning forked down viciously from the angry heavens and rain continued to fall, and there was no sanctuary for the man who had been hunted to the small remote town by the legendary bounty hunter.

Even darkness could not disguise the sheer power of the tall emaciated figure who clutched the grips of his matched Navy Colts firmly in his skeletal hands and stood watching the busy saloon. Iron Eyes stood like a statue in the centre of the wide street totally unaware of the rain that had been pounding down for more than three hours. But Iron Eyes had only been in the small border town of Cripple Creek for a mere ten minutes. He had informed the sheriff of his intentions and then wandered through the rain until he had located the Blue Garter saloon. This was the last saloon within the small six-street town.

With the tails of his long trail coat swaying in the evening breeze, Iron Eyes chewed on the end of his long-extinguished cigar and brooded. Spotting the distinctive dapple-grey mare tied up outside the noisy saloon, the bounty hunter suddenly knew that his prey was within spitting distance of his guns.

So close Iron Eyes imagined he could smell him.

Countless people had passed by the tall lethal figure, yet he had paid them no heed. He had only one thought in his mind and that was to kill the outlaw he knew was oblivious to his presence in Cripple Creek.

He had travelled fifty miles to administer his own brand of justice and lay claim to the $1,000 dollar reward money. Nothing but the price on the head of horse-thief Ben Drake could end this now.

Iron Eyes' long wet hair was hanging

lifelessly over his scarred features as the relentless rain beat down upon him. But he was like a puma stalking its next victim. He had his prey's scent in his flared nostrils and only death could stop him from completing what he had started a few days earlier.

The Wanted poster had said Dead or Alive. That was all the information Iron Eyes required to unleash his fury. Dead meant dead.

There was no other way.

His bony thumbs pulled back the hammers of his matched pistols until they locked fully into position.

Iron Eyes was now ready.

Ready to kill Ben Drake and anyone else who got in his way for that matter. Blood was his signature and he had signed his name throughout the West. Few lawmen ever questioned the tall bounty hunter before, during or after he had unleashed his venomous weaponry. If innocent people got killed whilst he was dishing out his lethal lead, nothing was ever said.

He was a law unto himself.

The tall ruthless bounty hunter strode across the muddy street and stepped up on to the boardwalk. He paused and stared over the swing-doors into the brightly illuminated bar room. He studied each of the men who were drinking and gambling with a coldness that was unique to the man known as a living ghost.

Then he recognized a face from the Wanted poster he had neatly folded in one of his deep pockets. The man was wearing a damp top coat and was seated near the back of the long bar next to a carpeted staircase.

That was Ben Drake, Iron Eyes thought.

Iron Eyes entered the saloon silently. Only his bloodstained spurs made any noise whatsoever. They jangled like the ominous knell of death.

The bounty hunter walked through the crowded room towards his goal. As he passed by the saloon's customers, every one of them stopped talking.

They had never seen anything remotely like this grisly apparition before.

By the time the bounty hunter had reached the round card-table where Drake was seated, the room was totally silent. Every soul within the Blue Garter just stood watching to see what the stranger in the long bloodstained coat would do next. They all gave a sigh of relief when they realized that it was not they whom the man with the Navy Colts in his hands was seeking, but Drake. It was if they were afraid to even breathe in Iron Eyes' presence, for fear of his deadly retribution.

The horse-thief looked up from his beer-glass and felt his jaw dropping until it touched his bandanna. Steam rose from Iron Eyes as if he were about to burst into flame. Drake gulped at the image that was glaring down at him through the strands of wet, dripping hair.

The burning eyes of the tall thin figure did not blink once as Iron Eyes raised both pistols until they were aiming straight at Ben Drake's head.

'Ben Drake?'

'I could be. Who the hell are you, stranger?' Drake asked meekly.

'The man who is gonna kill you, Drake,' came the low-pitched reply. 'They call me Iron Eyes.'

'Iron Eyes?' Drake's voice repeated the name in total disbelief. He knew of the bounty hunter who, it was said, could not be killed because he was already dead. 'Why do you want to kill little ol' me?'

'Why not?' Iron Eyes replied. 'You're a horse-thief and wanted dead or alive.'

'That don't mean ya have to kill me, Iron Eyes.' Drake tried to clear his throat of the dryness that suddenly filled it. 'I could walk with you to the sheriff's office. You'll still get the reward money.'

Iron Eyes had already noticed that Drake's left hand was out of sight beneath the round card-table.

'I don't work that way, Drake.'

'That's a crying shame,' the horse-thief said. 'For you!'

Ben Drake squeezed the trigger of the Remington that he had concealed in his left hand beneath the table. A bullet ripped through the wooden surface, sending splinters showering over the bounty hunter. The deadly lead ball skimmed the bounty hunter's temple. Iron Eyes felt blood tracing down his face.

Without a second's hesitation, both barrels of the matched Navy Colts blasted their lethal reply. What was left of the outlaw's head splattered over the wall behind the chair as the body fell on to the sawdust-covered floor.

Iron Eyes turned and faced the crowd. With blood covering half his face, he now looked even more horrific than usual.

'Can one of you bring me a bottle of rye?' he said, pushing his guns back into his belt.

The nervous bartender grabbed a bottle from the shelving beside the long mirror and cautiously walked to the tall bounty hunter. He handed him the whiskey.

'This OK?'

'It'll do.' Iron Eyes accepted the bottle and pulled the cork with his small razor-sharp teeth. He spat it away and then poured the fiery liquid over the bleeding gash on his temple. There was no sign that the strong liquor hurt the emotionless figure as it seared into the wound. Standing to his full imposing height, Iron Eyes drank what was left of the whiskey and then handed the empty bottle back to the nervous barkeep.

'How much do I owe you?' Iron Eyes asked, running his long fingers through his limp hair, revealing a face which had been victim to many battles.

'Nothing, friend,' came the quiet reply. 'It's on the house.'

'Much obliged.' Iron Eyes nodded.

'Did I hear right? Are you Iron Eyes?'

'Yep. Why?' Iron Eyes picked up a cigar from what was left of the card-table and placed it between his teeth. The bartender struck a match and lit the cigar. Iron Eyes inhaled deeply and savoured the strong smoke that filled his lungs.

'No reason.' The bartender swallowed hard. He had heard of the infamous bounty hunter but until now had thought the tales of the man who seemed more dead than alive were all made up. The sight before him was far more frightening than any of the stories he had heard told across his bar over the years.

Iron Eyes leaned over and grabbed the left foot of Ben Drake. He dragged the bleeding body through the sawdust down the length of the saloon.

The stunned, silent patrons watched the smoke trailing from the mouth of Iron Eyes as he dragged his prey out of the saloon.

3

Sheriff Tom Hardin had studied the strange bounty hunter for more than an hour as he waited patiently for the wire to arrive with confirmation from El Paso that would allow him to pay out the $1,000 reward money. With little remaining of Ben Drake's face and head, the sheriff had to verify the horse-thief's identity with the customers of the Blue Garter saloon.

That had been easy but the delay of waiting for El Paso to sanction the payment of the bounty seemed to take what was left of the night. Every second had felt like a lifetime to the balding law officer as he had waited with the ghostlike Iron Eyes in his drag office.

What unnerved the sheriff was that Iron Eyes just sat with the grips of his Navy Colts jutting from his belt. It was hard to tell if the man was asleep or awake for his eyes never fully closed. The eerie glare was haunting.

After an hour of nearly total silence, Iron Eyes had said little more than a half-dozen words. Each one had been barely audible and had merely responded to questions in the most economical fashion.

'You ought to get yourself a room in the hotel and rest up, Iron Eyes,' Hardin suggested. 'I figure that you ain't slept in a few days by the look of you.'

The eyes that were the colour of lead shot darted a glance across the room at the sheriff.

'I don't intend staying in this godforsaken town a second longer than it takes to get me my bounty,' Iron Eyes growled.

'The hotel rooms have got nice soft beds and for a few bucks extra you can get room service.' The sheriff raised both his eyebrows. 'If you get my drift?'

Iron Eyes shook his head.

'I ain't hungry.'

'That ain't exactly what I was getting

at.' Hardin sighed heavily. He wondered what kind of man Iron Eyes was, if he were a man at all. He had seen corpses that looked more alive than this infamous hunter of men. 'And there's the matter of you buying a new horse.'

'I got me a horse.'

'You have?' Hardin was confused.

'I got me a nice dapple-grey courtesy of Ben Drake.' Iron Eyes turned his head and stared at the office door as if he instinctively knew it would soon open.

The sound of footsteps running along the boardwalk echoed inside the sheriff's small office a few seconds before the door swung open. Joe Baker the telegraph man rushed in, crossed the room and handed a scrap of paper to the rotund lawman. Hardin searched his pockets vainly for his spectacles and then looked at the telegraph man.

'What's it say, Joe?' Hardin asked tiredly.

'You're supposed to read it yourself,' Baker said.

'If I knew where my gold rims were, I would,' Hardin snapped at the man. 'You already know what's in it, anyway. Read it to me.'

Joe Baker cleared his throat when he caught sight of the figure of Iron Eyes seated near the large window, staring out at the rising sun.

'It just says to pay the bounty, Tom.'

Iron Eyes stood and walked across the dismal office and leaned over the desk where Tom Hardin was sitting.

'Give me the money and I'll be going, Sheriff.'

Hardin felt his blood run cold when he stared up into the grim features of the man who still had dried blood covering half his face. Never in all his days had he set eyes upon a man who looked so ravished by life itself.

'I don't keep any money here. We'll have to wait for the bank to open up, Iron Eyes,' he informed the bounty hunter.

'How long will that be, Sheriff?' Iron Eyes whispered into the ear of the lawman.

18

'The bank opens at ten.' Hardin felt sweat trickling down the side of his face as terror filled his overweight body.

Iron Eyes looked up at the wall clock. It was nearly 5.36. His ice-cold stare returned to the seated man.

'I ain't waiting for another four or five hours.' There was something in the sheer tone of the voice that told the lawman he had better act and act quickly.

The sheriff gulped and rose slowly to his feet. He brushed past the telegraph man and then lifted his Stetson from the hatrack and placed it on his balding head. He turned the door-handle and signalled for both men to follow him out into the street.

They did.

The morning was cold after the storm of the previous night. The sun had yet to spread its warmth over the isolated town as its light snaked through the still-wet streets.

Iron Eyes watched the telegraph man make his way back to the office at the end of the main street as he trailed the sheriff down a side-street where the wooden houses had front gardens and picket fences. These were buildings of character and had obviously cost more than the rest of the dwellings in Cripple Creek put together.

'Where we headed, Sheriff?' Iron Eyes asked Hardin, who had paused outside the largest of the houses.

'This is the banker's house,' Hardin replied nodding, at the well-appointed structure which proved it paid to have money. Or at least access to other folks' money.

Iron Eyes leaned on the whitewashed fence and stared hard at the house. There was no sign of life.

'You figure this critter is honest, Sheriff?' Iron Eyes asked raising an eyebrow.

Hardin shrugged and pushed the gate open.

'Hell, he's a damn banker. They're all crooks, ain't they?'

Sheriff Hardin knocked on the solid wooden door for several fruitless minutes without being able to raise any of the house's occupants. Iron Eyes pulled one of his Navy Colts from his belt and cocked its hammer.

'What you doing, Iron Eyes?' Hardin asked.

The bounty hunter raised the pistol and aimed at the second-floor window.

'Waking the bastard up, Sheriff. Just waking the bastard up.'

The single shot shattered the window-pane of the banker's bedroom and the deafening noise echoed around the streets of Cripple Creek for several minutes.

'What the hell is going on down there?' Jed Smith, the banker, screamed through the shattered window. 'You better get out of here or I'll send for the sheriff.'

'This is the sheriff, Jed,' Hardin called back.

'Are you drunk?'

'I want you to open up the bank, Jed. We got to pay this gentleman some reward money,' the sheriff shouted up at the window.

'I open at ten, Sheriff,' Smith yelled back.

'I'd appreciate it if you'd open early today, Jed.' Hardin tried to appear calm but his eyes were fixed on the bounty hunter and the Navy Colt he held in his hand.

'Why should I?'

Faster than the sheriff could blink, Iron Eyes fanned his gun hammer several times and blasted every remaining pane of glass from the bedroom window. There was a long silence before the shaking voice of Jed Smith piped up again. 'I'll be right down, Tom.'

Hardin walked back to the bounty hunter and watched as the tall figure emptied the spent shells from his gun and replaced them with bullets from his deep coat-pockets. When the gun was loaded he pushed it back into his belt.

'You got his attention OK, Iron Eyes.' Hardin smiled broadly.

'I hate bankers. There ought to be Wanted posters out on the whole pack of them,' Iron Eyes growled. 'Dead or alive.'

Tom Hardin nodded. He actually agreed with Iron Eyes' blunt statement.

4

Iron Eyes had long known that it took a certain type of woman to look at his face without being racked with fear or revulsion. Even whores who were used to lying to their potential customers could not pretend that the sheer sight of his scarred face did not frighten them. In his entire life the infamous hunter had only encountered two females who seemed capable of looking straight at him and accepting what they saw. One had left without warning and the other had given her life to save his own.

It was with these memories that the tall bounty hunter stared in disbelief at the beautiful daughter of the banker as she walked arm in arm with her father along the quiet street ahead of the sheriff and himself.

Iron Eyes had been standing at the

gate when she had left the house and walked straight past him. She had looked straight at him without batting her long lashes.

The bounty hunter was intrigued.

He found it impossible to fathom how such a delicate young creature who had obviously been raised in the lap of luxury could have shown no emotions at all when looking at him.

Iron Eyes had seen hardened gunfighters turn their heads away from him rather than look for more than a few fleeting moments at his face.

Yet she seemed to be completely oblivious to the fact that Iron Eyes' face was unlike that of other men and that she ought to be frightened or sickened by it. Either that or she saw something within him that others failed to perceive.

The gaunt bounty hunter trailed the trio of respectable people to the bank and watched as Jed Smith unlocked the solid wooden doors with a massive brass key. Unlike any other building within the boundaries of Cripple Creek, the bank was constructed from stone blocks and had barred windows. It had been built to withstand even the most determined of attacks and looked as if its defences had never been breached.

Sheriff Hardin looked up at Iron Eyes and noticed something in his expression that he had not seen before. The man actually appeared to be interested in something apart from his reward money. Iron Eyes stood silently watching the young Rosie Smith as if she were the only person in the entire town worth looking at.

The beautiful girl was at least eighteen years of age and had the palest blue eyes that the bounty hunter had ever seen. Her soft blonde hair was draped on her shoulders the way single females always wore it. She stood motionless until her father had pushed the door open, then accepted his arm again and entered the interior of the large building.

'Young Rosie sure is a good-looking

gal, huh, Iron Eyes?' Hardin said to the hunter as the pair walked into the bank side by side.

Iron Eyes said nothing. He just watched as Jed Smith moved towards his safe and turned the dial. Rosie Smith was seated near one of the large windows. The morning sunlight cascaded over her and drew Iron Eyes to her like a moth to a flame.

As Iron Eyes' mule-ear boots approached her over the marble floor, the sound of his spurs echoed around the bank foyer. Her head tilted backwards and she smiled. The bounty hunter had not seen anyone smile at him for as long as he could remember. He stopped in his tracks.

'Why does my father have to pay you, sir?' Rosie asked innocently.

Iron Eyes seemed confused by the question.

'Because I killed an outlaw, ma'am.'

Her smile faded.

'You killed a man? Why?'

'He tried to kill me first.' Iron Eyes pointed at the still-raw gash on his temple. 'He came damn close, too.'

'You must be a bounty hunter.'

'Yep. That's what I am.'

Rosie Smith lowered her head thoughtfully. 'It seems a very dangerous occupation.'

'That's right, ma'am.' Iron Eyes turned and walked back to the old sheriff who was now leaning on the mahogany bank-counter watching the paper money being counted out.

'One thousand dollars exactly, Iron Eyes,' Hardin said.

'I don't take paper money. Make it golden eagles or silver coin,' Iron Eyes said bluntly, pushing the notes back at the banker whilst still looking at the man's daughter as she stood near the window.

'You want golden eagles?' Smith asked coyly.

'Or silver twenty-dollar coins.' Iron Eyes rubbed his brow and felt the torn skin. It was still raw and angry but no longer bleeding.

Sheriff Hardin made a pained expression at the banker. Smith nodded and returned to the safe with the paper money in his hands.

'This won't take long, Rosie,' Smith called out to his daughter.

'I'm in no hurry, Father,' she replied.

'Don't you like paper money?' Hardin asked the tall man.

'Nope. It catches fire.'

'But you like her, don't you, son?' Hardin had a twinkle in his eye.

Iron Eyes continued to watch the beautiful female who stared across the bank in their direction. She was smiling again.

'Yep. I like her,' he admitted.

5

Iron Eyes secured the leather laces of his saddle-bags behind the cantle and then stepped into the stirrup. His long right leg cleared the large dapple-grey's broad back easily. He patted the bags and took pleasure in the sound of the golden eagles within one of the satchels.

'Where you headed, Iron Eyes?' Sheriff Hardin asked the bounty hunter.

'Sanora, over the border in Mexico,' came the crisp reply.

'Why there?'

Iron Eyes pulled the neatly folded wanted poster out of one of his deep trail-coat pockets and opened it up until the photographic image of a man called Black Ben Tucker stared up at him. He waved the poster at the sheriff.

'This bastard has an even two thousand dollars on his head, Sheriff.'

'A tidy sum.'

'Enough to keep me in bullets and whiskey.' Iron Eyes sighed, forcing the poster back into the pocket of his coat.

Sheriff Hardin leaned on the wooden upright outside his office and wondered what drove a man like this one. Why would anyone choose to risk everything in pursuit of the bounty upon other men's heads?

'Why do you do this, son?'

'Do what?' Iron Eyes tilted his head and stared down at the lawman.

'Risk your life and get yourself shot up.'

'I'm a hunter, Sheriff,' Iron Eyes explained. 'I've always been a hunter. First it was critters and then it became outlaws. It's what I do. I don't do nothing else.'

'But what if you get yourself killed?'

Iron Eyes forced a smile.

'I once tracked a man for three hundred miles and finally caught up with him. I killed the varmint and then the town marshal decided he wasn't gonna pay me the reward money.'

'What did ya do?' Hardin looked at the repellent horseman with curiosity.

'I got angry.' Iron Eyes gathered up his reins. 'Then I got even.'

'How do you know this Tucker's in Sanora, Iron Eyes?' Hardin asked the bounty hunter.

'I have my spies. He's in Sanora OK.' Iron Eyes hauled the neck of the dapple-grey around and sank his spurs into its flesh. The horse responded instantly and galloped along the now dry main street of Cripple Creek.

The dapple-grey felt its reins being drawn back as its new master steered it down the quiet, well-tended street that held the best-appointed houses in the small town, the best of which belonged to the banker and his daughter.

Iron Eyes eased the mount to a walk and stared at the banker's house with a curiosity which was totally alien to him. Two men were already repairing the window-panes of Jed Smith's bedroom. One was up a ladder whilst the other remained at the foot of it keeping it steady. Their faces went deathly pale as the ghostlike rider allowed his new horse to walk slowly past the gate.

Then Iron Eyes spotted the young female who had intrigued him earlier that morning. Rosie Smith sat on a whitewashed swing rocking herself back and forth. She seemed totally unaware of anything around her. She was singing quietly to herself the way people do when afraid others might hear.

Iron Eyes eased his horse to a halt and listened to the sweet young voice. He had not heard anything so pure in all his long days.

Her back was to the rider but she seemed to hear his horse's hoofs prancing on the ground outside her garden. She stopped singing.

Iron Eyes suddenly felt as if he had intruded on something that was not meant for his ears.

Before the lovely Rosie Smith had time to rise from the swing and turn in his direction, Iron Eyes had spurred his mount and ridden at top speed away from the quiet scene.

Within a minute he was out on the desolate range and headed south towards the border. Iron Eyes knew that there was another prize for him to claim in the sleepy Mexican town of Sanora.

But try as he might, the bounty hunter seemed unable to keep his mind on the man known as Black Ben Tucker. All he could think about was the golden-haired girl who had stared at his face and shown no sign of fear or distaste.

Iron Eyes could not understand why Rosie Smith had wasted one of her precious smiles upon his unworthy countenance. Had he at last met the one girl who saw beyond his scarred features and actually liked what had lain hidden from everyone else for so very long?

Had she actually liked what she had seen?

Iron Eyes drove the dapple-grey on as if trying to outride his own thoughts.

Yet even with his matted hair flapping over the collar of his trail-coat like the wings of a bat, Iron Eyes knew there were some things it was impossible to escape from.

One's own imagination being one of them.

6

The six Mexican bandits crossed the shallow river and stopped their lathered-up mounts beneath the canopy of a massive Texan oak-tree. The air tasted sweeter on this side of the border because they knew there were far richer souls here whom they could torment with their own brand of evil.

Without even having to be told, the riders checked that their weapons were fully loaded. Each man knew exactly where they were headed and what they were about to do.

The self-proclaimed leader of the ruthless gang of bandits was called simply Malverez. His followers had new names almost every day of the week, but not the bloodthirsty Malverez. He did not worry about who knew his true identity because anyone who did, had very little time left to live.

They were a motley bunch to look at and no mistake. But that was more by design than circumstance. For they were probably the most successful bandits to drift back and forth across the Texas-Mexico border.

Few gave them a second look and that was their strength. How could anyone describe people who masterfully blended into any background?

Like the very air itself, they seemed to be totally unseen and unnoticed.

For a decade, the bandits had tried their hands at every known crime but it had been abduction at which they excelled. Almost by accident the half-dozen killers had found the one crime that appeared to offer them the highest rewards for the least risk. They had perfected the art of allowing their victims to bring them what they wanted by the simple ruse of kidnapping their offspring.

Malverez and his men had managed to strike more than thirty times over a decade and to extort more than

$50,000 from their victims' loved ones. With cold-blooded expertise the six bandits ensured they were never identified by those they preyed upon. Without exception, they killed everyone who had ever fallen victim to their cruel crimes.

Without eye-witnesses, they were safe.

So they killed and killed.

It was so easy.

For these were men who did not display their wealth, as some would have been unable to resist doing. They remained unwashed and able to do their evil deeds unhindered by the law on both sides of the Rio Grande.

They were, to all intents and purposes, merely drifting Mexican *vaqueros*. They had yet to be branded with their crimes.

Until they were, they were as free as the air they breathed.

They aimed their mounts north and headed for the town that they knew boasted a well-established bank filled to overflowing with cattle-ranchers' money.

But they would not rob the bank.

That was a deed that they knew would bring the law down on them faster than they could ride back to their Mexican hideout. They would let the banker take the money from his safe and bring it to them himself.

He would do so willingly because he was the father of a beautiful daughter. Such men would do anything they were told to have their daughter returned unharmed. They could not even imagine that they might be betrayed, for such unthinkable things do not enter the minds of good people.

Good people blindly accept the word of others. To even contemplate being double-crossed was something that they could never accept as even the remotest of possibilities.

But Malverez had no such problem with morality.

The six bandits had visited Cripple Creek many times, finding out everything they needed to know about the banker, in order to execute their daring plan.

Jed Smith would willingly strip every

dollar from his bank and bring it to them without question, just to have his beautiful blonde daughter returned to him safely.

That was the one thing all decent souls had in common and the bandits relied upon. They assumed everyone shared their own code of ethics.

But Malverez and his men would not keep their side of the bargain. They would kill the daughter and the banker and ride away with the loot.

This was the way they always worked, the way that Malverez and his cronies kept themselves one step ahead of the law and the hangman's noose.

Malverez ensured that they never left any loose ends.

The six bandits were riding hard for the remote border town of Cripple Creek when they spotted the distant horseman astride the dapple-grey. Iron Eyes held his mount in check directly ahead of them.

Malverez raised his arm and stopped his followers.

7

It was a horrific vision which faced the Mexican bandits on the narrow trail. The gaunt rider astride the skittish mount bore little resemblance to other men. His long black hair flapped on the morning breeze as his eyes narrowed and stared coldly at the men who drew cautiously closer.

Iron Eyes pulled his dapple-grey mount's head back and studied the six riders directly ahead of him along the well-used trail. He pulled one of his Navy Colts from his belt and cocked its hammer in readiness.

Holding the pistol across his belly, the bounty hunter held his horse firmly in check until the riders slowed up in front of him, stopping their lathered-up mounts a mere twenty feet from the nose of his snorting animal.

Iron Eyes chewed on the end of his

cigar silently. These were men who made the bounty hunter feel uneasy. They were dressed like peasants but he had never seen so many expensive pistols adorning so many unworthy hips before.

They were not what they seemed, and he knew it.

The half-dozen bandits stared at the strange rider who was blocking their way towards the town of Cripple Creek. It was Malverez who edged his horse forward first and grinned broadly at the bounty hunter.

'We wish you no harm, *señor*.'

'That's lucky for you,' Iron Eyes said coldly. 'I'd hate to have to kill you all.'

Malverez glanced at the cocked pistol in the rider's hand and shrugged.

'Why do you hold a gun on us? We are simple *vaqueros* looking for honest work.'

Iron Eyes raised an eyebrow.

'You ain't wanted. I'd know them faces if I'd ever seen them on Wanted posters, friend. But I don't think you're simple *vaqueros*.'

Malverez felt the hairs on his neck rising as sweat trickled down his back. He had no desire to tangle with anyone who looked as dangerous as the horseman before him. A man who was obviously more than capable of honouring his threats.

'Are you a bounty hunter, *amigo*?'

Iron Eyes stared hard at the bandit leader.

'Yep. I'm a bounty hunter. Does that trouble you?'

Malverez smiled. 'An honest man does not fear anything.'

Iron Eyes glanced around the faces of the sheepish men who flanked Malverez. None of them seemed willing to look up from beneath his straw sombrero.

'I got me a feeling that you men are more than you pretend to be, but if there ain't a bounty on your heads, it don't much concern me.' The bounty hunter allowed his mount to walk to the side of the trail without taking his eyes off any of them.

One of the bandits drew his pistol from its expensive holster and tried to aim at the skeletal rider.

Iron Eyes swiftly lifted his Navy Colt and squeezed its trigger. The bullet tore through the hand of the bandit sending the gun flying high into the air.

'That was a stupid thing to do. I ought to kill the lot of you,' Iron Eyes growled.

Malverez waved his hands around frantically. 'Please, *señor*. Do not kill us. My friend is a fool.'

The bounty hunter drew his other pistol and cocked both hammers at once. He trained the weapons on the six men.

'Drop them guns, boys,' he ordered.

'Do as he says, *amigos*,' Malverez instructed his men.

The riders peeled their guns from their holsters and dropped them to the ground. Malverez carefully picked his own pistol from his holster with his index finger and thumb and let it fall to the ground.

'What is your name, *señor?*'

'They call me Iron Eyes.'

Malverez nodded. He had heard the tales of the infamous bounty hunter and knew that they were lucky to be alive still.

'I have heard of you, *amigo.*'

'Many men have.' Iron Eyes waved his guns at the bandit. 'I've killed most of the ones who have, though.'

'Please excuse my hot-headed friend, Señor Iron Eyes. He is most ignorant.' Malverez knew that if there was one man who could stop his small group of bandits from completing their chosen task, he was looking straight at him.

'The next time our paths cross, I hope you'll remember all them stories about me,' Iron Eyes said coldly. 'Because they're all true. If any of you varmints cross my path again, I'll kill you all, even if you ain't worth a dime.'

'But why would a famous bounty hunter kill innocent men when there is no profit in it?' the bandit leader asked.

'Because I like killing, friend. It's

what I do best.' Iron Eyes chewed on the unlit butt of his cigar and turned the dapple-grey away from the motley group of riders. He spurred his horse and rode past them towards the distant river and the Mexican border.

Malverez dismounted and picked up his gun as his men did the same.

'Why did we not just kill him?' the bandit with the bleeding bullet-hole in his hand asked angrily.

Malverez slid his pistol into its hand-tooled holster. 'You cannot kill this gringo so easy, *amigo*. They say that he is already dead.'

8

Iron Eyes had spotted the ten Apache braves to his right a few minutes after he had crossed the shallow fast-flowing river and made his way deep into the Mexican countryside. They had appeared silently high above the trail and rode in single file, watching his every movement. Every so often the lead rider would disappear behind the ridge and then reappear at the rear of the line of Apache horsemen.

Iron Eyes did not like being followed so blatantly but knew that that was the way of the Plains Indian. They liked to torment their prey before striking. The brush was sparse here and there were too many narrow gulches for his liking.

A perfect place for an ambush, he thought.

Iron Eyes recognized the distinctive broad, colourful headbands wrapped around the skulls of the braves, holding their long black manes of hair in check. The yellow paint across their noses only confirmed the bounty hunter's worst fears. These were the Ochawa Apache and they were a long way from their home up in the Arizona territories.

They were also the most deadly of all the Apache people he had ever had the misfortune of running into. Like himself, they seemed to enjoy killing for killing's sake and did not require any excuse to start doing so.

Iron Eyes had encountered Ochawa braves before and knew they were not to be trusted. He had killed many of their kind in the past when they had attacked him for simply being on their land. The Ochawa were far more dangerous than any other Apache tribe he had encountered.

He still bore the scars of their last meeting.

Iron Eyes nursed the dapple-grey along the dried-up creek-bed and kept his head tilted so that he could see where his observers were at all times.

The blazing sun bounced off the metal tips of the war-lances which were secured to the necks of their ponies with rawhide. The flashes danced down over the troubled Iron Eyes as he continued to ride slowly along the well-used trail. Unlike most Apache, the Ochawa seemed to relish displaying their vivid colours for all to see. They had rifles wrapped in beaded sheaths resting on their thighs as they steered their painted ponies along the top of the sandy ridge.

The Ochawa knew that they could demoralize most of their enemies by their sheer presence. It was a ploy that had worked on all their foes except Iron Eyes. He was not impressed by anything except an opponent's skill. Unfortunately the Ochawa also had this in abundance.

Iron Eyes knew that his reputation amongst the numerous tribes of Apache had made his head a prized trophy that few could resist trying to collect.

With the dried-up river-bed winding its way through the ever-narrowing ridges of white sand that flanked the rider, the bounty hunter knew that his time was running out and the Apache braves above him would soon attack.

An arrow landed a few feet in front of the dapple-grey but Iron Eyes sank his spurs into its flesh and forced it to continue.

Then he noticed that a few of the Ochawa had disappeared from the ridge leaving only seven braves in the silent line of riders. This time the bounty hunter instinctively knew that the warriors would not return to their fellow braves but come charging out at him from any of the dozens of hiding-places along the narrow trail. Iron Eyes carefully raised his left hand and pulled the handle of one of his Navy Colts from his belt.

His thumb cocked the hammer of the pistol and rested it on top of the saddle horn.

Iron Eyes did not have time to

wonder where or when the Indians would attack. Suddenly, the three Ochawa who had peeled off the main group galloped from around a corner in front of the dapple-grey.

The deafening screams made the powerful horse rear up and kick out at its attackers as Iron Eyes raised his pistol and fired point blank at the lead rider. The brave was sent headlong off the back of the painted pony and landed at the hoofs of one of the trailing mounts.

The second pony went down, sending its rider crashing into the white sand.

Iron Eyes blasted his gun again when he heard the sound of the rifles being cocked above him. Deadly bullets flashed through the afternoon air, tearing up the ground all around the grim-faced bounty hunter. Iron Eyes fought to control his terrified horse as the seven other Ochawa came charging down from the ridge.

Luckily for the bounty hunter, their

rifles were single-shot Springfields, probably captured from a raid on a cavalry fortress somewhere up in the distant territories of Arizona. Even for well-trained troopers, it was no easy task to control a horse and reload the carbines.

The dapple-grey swung full circle as its master fired his pistol in all directions at his attackers.

Gunsmoke filled the narrow gulch, making it impossible to see all of his enemies clearly. Iron Eyes dropped the empty gun into his deep left pocket, then hauled the other Navy Colt from his belt.

Without even thinking, Iron Eyes spurred his grey straight at the descending Apache braves. His long arm thrashed out at the riders frantically. He could feel the impact of his gun barrel as it smashed into one skull after another whilst he forced the strong horse up the sandy incline.

Iron Eyes did not want to waste a single shot on these warriors because he knew that he would not have any time to reload. Every shot had to count and there were only six bullets in the chambers of the Navy Colt.

Reaching the top of the ridge, the rider pulled back on his reins and turned the grey mount around to survey what was left of his attackers.

An arrow swept out of the gunsmoke and hit him squarely in his left leg just below the knee. He felt his leg being pinned to the thick fender of his saddle.

The horse reared up when Iron Eyes blasted at the remaining Indians who were attempting to ride up through the soft sand of the ridge. He did not waste time counting how many fell from the backs of their painted ponies.

Iron Eyes sank his spurs into the dapple-grey and thundered off into the depths of the Mexican sand-dunes. He had no idea whether the Ochawa were chasing him. All he could think about was the arrow that had pinned his leg to the saddle fender. He had to find a place where he could extract the shaft of wood and stop the bleeding.

The dapple-grey stopped when Iron Eyes was convinced that the Indians had not continued following him into the barren wastes of the Mexican heartland. The rider reached back to his saddle-bags, opened one of the satchel flaps and extracted a half-bottle of whiskey. He pulled the cork from its neck and raised the bottle to his dry mouth. He swallowed a quarter of its fiery contents.

The pain in his innards now matched the one in his leg.

Iron Eyes stared down at his leg and the distinctive feathered flight on the arrow which had skewered his calf muscle to the leather fender.

He gritted his teeth and poured some of the whiskey sparingly down into his boot. He could feel the liquor burning the bleeding flesh. Iron Eyes knew he would not be able to dismount until he had pulled the arrow out of his saddle leather.

He dropped the bottle into his trail-coat pocket, held on to the shaft of the arrow and pulled at it hard. He could feel its metal point coming out of the thick leather of his saddle. Iron Eyes carefully dismounted.

He sat down on the sand and stared at the arrow which had driven its way through his boot and leg. Blood dripped from the arrowhead.

Iron Eyes slid his long Bowie knife from its hiding-place inside his right boot and stared at its razor-sharp blade. He carefully cut the arrowhead off the wooden shaft and tossed it away. Iron Eyes pulled one of the many bullets from the same deep trail-coat pocket and used his knife to lever the lead ball free of the brass casing.

After cutting a small groove in the wooden shaft of the arrow the bounty hunter poured the black powder into it.

Iron Eyes located a long cigar in his vest and placed it between his sharp teeth. He struck a match and cupped the flame to the tip of the cigar. He inhaled deeply, removed the cigar from his mouth and blew at the white ash until only the glowing red of its fiery heart could be seen.

Iron Eyes knew that the Ochawa often tipped their arrowheads with snake venon; he had no other choice but to try to burn the poison out.

Holding firmly on to the arrow shaft with his left hand, Iron Eyes lowered the smouldering cigar-tip over the gunpowder-filled groove which pro-truded from his calf. He ignited the powder, and dragged the blood-coated arrow from his leg at exactly the same time; the ghostly figure felt the burning powder move through his calf muscle.

Any normal man would have passed out, but Iron Eyes refused to be like other men. He refused to acknowledge the pain that tore through him.

Iron Eyes propped himself up against the sand-dune and stared at the smoke drifting from the arrow holes on either side of his left boot. He bent forward and pulled the boot free of his leg and then poured the blood away.

Chewing on his cigar and staring through the smoke, Iron Eyes picked up the whiskey bottle again. He thought about pouring some of its contents over his smouldering leg but then decided to drink it instead.

The liquor burned its way down into his innards. It made the bounty hunter reel back and look straight up into the blinding sun.

Yet again he had somehow survived.

His thoughts drifted between the beautiful Rosie Smith back in Cripple Creek and the man he had been told was holed up in Sanora.

A man he wanted to kill for the price on his head.

Iron Eyes pulled his boot back on and then grabbed at his reins hanging from the bridle of the dapple-grey. He pulled himself off the sand-dune. He leaned over the saddle and stared out into the shimmering heat haze.

He was hurting and angry.

9

Sanora was a sleepy town of more than a hundred whitewashed adobes resting thirty miles south of the border. Their red-tiled roof-tops could be seen from twenty miles away in any direction amid the white sandy terrain. This was a place where people came to drink, sleep and hide.

Men like Tucker. Black Ben Tucker dressed entirely in black and rode a stallion to match. His was a charmed life but he knew exactly where to head when it had become too hot for him in Texas. He had aimed his trusty mount at the border and headed for Sanora.

He had ridden here because he wanted a safe haven where he could spend the money he had made from his last job, unhindered by the Texan lawmen who were hunting him. He was a train-robber who had only one equal and that was the legendary Jesse James. But unlike James, who had a large gang, Tucker worked entirely alone.

He had managed to steal more than $10,000 from the Southern Pacific Railroad a few months earlier but found his every turn blocked by the Texas Rangers.

Riding with the law dogging his tail, Black Ben had decided that it was far healthier to head south of the border and disappear rather than wait for the inevitable.

For nearly two weeks the famed robber had rested amid the peaceful Mexican surroundings spending his newly acquired fortune on wine, women and song. He had decided that once he had had his fill of these he would cut across country and head into Southern California. From there he could head up the coast to the gold fields. There were plenty of trains there shipping not only money around but gold ore. A man of his talents could make a lot more money there than by remaining in Texas.

Black Ben Tucker knew that the Texas Rangers would not venture into Mexico in order to capture him. They had rules which made it impossible. But Tucker had no idea that there was another man who was trailing him to the sleepy Mexican town.

A dangerous man who did not live by the rules of others. A wounded man who followed the tracks of his prey wherever they led.

Iron Eyes did not recognize any man-made borders.

He went wherever he liked to claim the bounty upon the heads of those who were wanted dead or alive.

Even with blood running freely down inside his left boot, Iron Eyes had continued his quest for the man with the $2,000 bounty on his head. At first he had not noticed the delirium which confused his usually keen mind and slowly overwhelmed him. Iron Eyes had been riding for more than an hour since the Indian attack but could not remember any of the miles that now lay behind him.

Only dogged determination had brought him here to capture the outlaw whose trail had led him into this hell-hole.

The strong dapple-grey beneath his saddle galloped into Sanora just before two o'clock on the hot afternoon. The bounty hunter stared at the dozens of men who sat with their backs against the whitewashed adobe walls and slept beneath their sombreros. They lined both sides of the quiet Sanora streets as Iron Eyes pulled back on his reins and slowed the powerful horse to a walk.

The bounty hunter felt sweat running down his face. He was burning up and his leg throbbed with every movement of the tall horse. Yet there seemed to be nobody awake to notice that the wounded rider was swaying on his saddle.

He had made it to this remote town but it had cost him a hefty price in blood. Iron Eyes knew that the arrow that he had pulled from his leg must have been tipped with poison because he had lost blood before and not felt like this. Poison must have entered his body and was now wreaking its toll upon him.

Iron Eyes had never felt truly at ease in Mexico during the hours of siesta. It did not seem natural to the bounty hunter for people to sleep during the hours of daylight. Now with a fever raging inside his confused mind, Iron Eyes imagined that the sleeping people were only pretending and would rise up and start shooting at him at any moment.

Yet the bounty hunter could not manage to find either of his trusty Navy Colts. His hands could barely hold on to the leather reins any longer.

The heavy-lidded eyes wandered aimlessly around the sleeping towns-people as he stopped the horse outside one of the many cantinas and slid from his saddle. Hanging on to the saddle horn with every ounce of his strength, Iron Eyes stared at the beaded curtain that swayed before him.

Black Ben Tucker strolled out into the blazing sun and looked at the tall emaciated figure.

Their eyes met. A few seconds later, the bounty hunter crashed into the sun-baked ground at Tucker's feet.

10

Being so close to the border, there was nothing unusual in seeing Mexican riders drifting in and out of Cripple Creek. Malverez knew that they would not warrant a second look from even the most curious of the town's citizens. As the chimes of the town hall clock struck two and echoed around Cripple Creek, the six bandits rode their exhausted mounts through the quiet streets as if shielded by a cloak of invisibility.

They were slumped in their saddles and spaced just far enough apart to give any onlookers the impression that they were not together at all.

Malverez dismounted outside the Blue Garter saloon and watched as his men drifted to various other buildings. They tied their horses up beside six different water-troughs along the long main street and moved around the quiet streets giving the appearance of men who were just passing through the remote Texan town, men who had never met before.

They did not have to work too hard because it seemed that no one gave them a second look anyway. As the bandit leader had guessed, mere Mexican drifters were not worthy of a second glance.

This was the ace in Malverez's pack.

One by one the bandits slowly made their way to a small cantina which was tucked away in a small alley just off the main street.

The men entered separately a few minutes apart, and gathered in a dark corner of the building. They stared at the wall clock perched above the flaming cooking range from which savoury smells arose.

It was a few minutes after two in the afternoon.

They had arrived exactly on time, just as Malverez had planned, even though they had been delayed by the strange bounty hunter near the wide river crossing.

The bandits made their way to two separate tables and then ordered chilli and wine. When the waitress was out of earshot the men talked and honed the details of their despicable plan until each knew exactly what he had to do, and when he had to do it.

Malverez went over and over every aspect of his plan. The bandits listened and nodded.

Timing was the key factor for the men who lived by destroying the dreams of others. Everything had to be timed to the nearest second and the six bandits all synchronized their pocket-watches until they ticked as one.

Previous scouting visits to Cripple Creek had given the six men details of Jed Smith and his daughter that were invaluable to their plan. They knew the banker's habits even better than he knew them himself. They also knew where Smith lived and the swiftest way to and from the large house. Every detail of the banker's daily routine was etched into the bandits minds.

Jed Smith was a creature of habit and never deviated from his habitual routine. The bandits knew when he would leave the bank for his mid morning break, and where he went to have exactly two cups of black sugarless coffee. They knew that however busy his bank was, Smith would leave at exactly two minutes after one by a side door and walk home for his lunch, leaving his staff to cope.

The bandits knew that Smith would leave his home at ten minutes before two and call in at the Blue Garter saloon for exactly two glasses of whiskey before returning to his bank at just after two in the afternoon.

Jed Smith would lock the door to the bank at four and his staff would leave at precisely five. At 5.30 he would leave by the bank's large front doors and make his way home, again via the Blue Garter saloon. He would arrive at his home between 6.15 and 6.30. They also knew that Smith's daughter never went anywhere without her father and whilst he worked, she would remain in or around her home alone. A cleaning lady would spend an hour between nine and ten each morning and not return to Smith's home until the following day.

It was a routine that never deviated by more than a few seconds on any day and this was why Malverez knew how easy their job was going to be.

They would fill their bellies in the cantina and then put the first part of their plan into operation.

11

It was exactly four in the afternoon. Each of their pocket watches chimed as one within their silver cases. Malverez had organized everything down to the last second. The bandit pulled up outside the home of Jed and Rosie Smith atop a newly purchased four-horse wagon with three of his men sitting on the flat-bed. Four of their mounts were tied up to the tail-gate whilst the remaining pair of ruthless Mexicans were on the other side of Cripple Creek watching their pocket-watches and waiting for the precise moment when they too had to act.

Malverez pushed his right foot down hard on the long brake-pole and dragged the heavy reins back until he was able to wrap them around the pole. The team of horses instinctively knew that they were not going anywhere until the bandit wished them to do so.

Dust swirled over the scene masking the details of the four men's actions from prying eyes. But the bandits knew what their jobs entailed and could have executed them with their own eyes closed.

But their eyes were not closed. They were wide open and aware of everything. Without a second's hesitation the four bandits jumped down from the wagon, leapt over the white picket fence and entered the garden. Before anyone in the street had time to part their lace drapes and look out of their windows to see what was happening, the men had all entered the large house.

They were like a well-oiled machine as they moved through the large building, room by room.

But they had done this so many times before that it had become almost second nature to the bandits. They knew how to take their victims by surprise and did so without any sign of emotion.

If Rosie Smith had managed to scream out, the bandits might have been forced to abandon their plans and hightail it out of Cripple Creek. But Rosie had not had time to even catch her breath when the four men stormed the house. Malverez had kicked the front door open and made his way into the large house at the same time as his three companions came in through the rear door.

Rosie Smith had not even been able to open her mouth when the filthy hand grabbed at her face and hauled her on to the expensive carpet.

'She is most pretty, *amigo*,' one of the bandits had said, laughing as he held her face down on the floor whilst the bandit leader tied her wrists and ankles together with wet rawhide.

The bandit who was still nursing the bullet-hole in his right hand knelt on Rosie Smith's back as Malverez tied a blindfold over her eyes and then rammed his greasy bandanna into her unsuspecting mouth before securing it with a tight knot.

'There will be time for pleasure when we get her over the border and to our hideout, Jose,' Malverez snapped, dragging the helpless female off the floor as if she was a rag-doll.

The remaining fourth bandit tore the velvet drapes from one of the front windows and wrapped it around their shocked victim until she completely vanished inside the heavy material.

A matter of seconds later all four men lifted up their precious bundle, marched swiftly into the front garden and out to the quiet street. They tossed the helpless Rosie on to the flat-bed of the wagon and closed the tail-gate. Malverez secured it and then nodded to the other bandits.

'You know what to do, *amigos*.' The bandit leader ran to the front wheel of the wagon, climbed up to the driver's seat and released the brake-pole. Malverez whipped the heavy reins down hard on to the backs of the team of horses.

Having untied their three mounts from the rear of the flat-bed wagon, leaving only Malverez's mount, the bandits quickly threw themselves on to their saddles and rode back to the main street of Cripple Creek.

Their job was not finished.

If anyone in the adjoining houses had seen the men they would never have known what lay hidden inside the velvet drapes that they had thrown into the back of the wagon. Who would have even guessed that the innocent daughter of Jed Smith could have been hidden inside the luxurious fabric?

But there were no eyewitnesses fast enough to catch even a glimpse of the men.

The bandits had gone and left only a cloud of dust in their wake in the quiet side street.

The entire operation had taken less than one hundred seconds from beginning to end.

Now the bandits had disappeared.

Malverez whipped the team of horses

up to speed and knew that the first part of his ruthless plan had gone smoothly. Looking at his pocket-watch as he drove the horses out of Cripple Creek, Malverez knew that his men were about to put the next carefully timed part of his plan into action.

The speeding four-horse wagon thundered out on to the dusty trail with the skilled hands of the bandit leader gripping the heavy reins firmly. Malverez glanced over his shoulder quickly before returning his attention to the twisting dirt road ahead of him.

Cripple Creek had disappeared in the plume of dust behind him.

12

It was five after four. Malverez and his men had already executed their plan and brutally abducted the beautiful Rosie Smith. The two remaining bandits had been waiting for the banker to lock up the Cripple Creek bank before delivering the note that their leader had painstakingly written by hand. The two bandits waited at either end of the street watching the large window to see if it had been accepted and understood. They watched their three comrades riding past them. The riders each took a different route out of the town, but would meet up again across the border.

Jed Smith had only just escorted the last of their customers off the premises and locked the solid doors of his bank when he heard something tapping against them. The sound stopped the man in his tracks. The banker turned and stared at the piece of paper which had been slipped beneath the doors.

'What on earth is that?' Smith asked aloud, thinking that one of the customers had accidentally dropped a receipt.

His two cashiers had walked across the marble flooring towards Smith as he bent down, picked up the paper and unfolded it. His eyes darted back and forth as he silently read the message.

'Anything important, Mr Smith?' head cashier Clayton Nash asked his boss as Bobby Cooper the junior clerk looked on curiously.

Smith's face went pale.

'What is it, sir?' Cooper asked.

Smith did not reply to either man. He just stared at the words which had been written in capital letters upon the paper. His blood seemed to freeze in his veins as he tried desperately to fathom whether his tired eyes had actually read the brief message correctly. Smith hurriedly walked away from his two employees towards his office without answering.

His footsteps resounded around the bank.

The sound of the office door being closed behind him echoed within the large foyer of the bank as Jed Smith entered his private sanctuary. Sweat was now tracing down his face as panic gripped him by the throat.

'This cannot be happening,' Smith muttered in a vain attempt to convince himself that he was imagining this whole thing, which had brought him face to face with his worst nightmare.

He was still shaking as he sat at his desk and read the note again.

DEAR MR SMITH

WE HAVE TAKEN YOUR DAUGHTER, WE WILL KILL HER UNLESS YOU BRING US $50,000. WE WILL CONTACT YOU TOMORROW AND GIVE YOU DETAILS OF WHERE YOU HAVE TO BRING MONEY. DO NOT TELL THE LAW. IF YOU AGREE TO PAY FOR YOUR

DAUGHTERS LIFE, PLACE A LAMP IN THE BANK WINDOW.

YOUR FRIEND.

The words could not have been plainer. His daughter had been kidnapped and was being held for ransom. Jed Smith had always feared that one day armed robbers would raid and rob his bank but he had never once imagined that someone would kidnap his beloved Rosie to get what they wanted.

Why pick on her?

What sort of person would pick on a helpless female when they could face a man?

Jed Smith knew that he was probably dealing with a coward or cowards. But they might just be sick enough to kill her if he did not comply with their wishes.

There came a knock on the door of his office. Smith glanced up from the scrap of paper but could not make out who was standing behind the frosted glass. His eyes were filled with tears.

'Mr Smith?'

The banker recognized the voice of Clayton Nash. He rubbed his eyes dry with the white handkerchief he always wore in his breast-pocket.

'Come in, Clayton.'

Nash opened the door and looked at the seated figure. He knew that something was very wrong.

'Can I help you, sir?'

Smith gave a huge sigh and buried his head in his hands. The sound of sobbing filled the entire bank.

Nash slowly crossed the office and stood beside the man he had worked for for nearly twenty years.

'What is it, Jed?'

Smith wiped his eyes but it seemed that the handkerchief was not capable of coping with the flood of tears that flowed from his swollen eyes.

'Yes, Clayton. You can help me.'

'Anything, sir.'

'Place a lamp in the large window,'

Smith managed to say.

'Yes, sir.' Clayton Nash cleared his own throat and walked out of the office. He was not going to question the banker any further. It was obvious that the sobbing man had already reached breaking point.

The two bandits watched the lamp being placed in the largest of the bank's impressive windows, then casually mounted their horses. Neither acknowledged the other and they rode out of town by separate routes.

They now had to inform Malverez that Jed Smith had taken the bait and was doing exactly as their leader had instructed. The trail dust drifted over the street as Clayton Nash and Bobby Cooper left the bank by the side door. For the first time since either man had worked in the prosperous bank, they were being allowed off work early.

The younger of the two, Cooper, did not ask any questions and ran home but Clayton Nash was made uneasy by the behaviour of Smith since he had received the note.

He made his way straight to the sheriff's office. Standing on the board-walk outside the grubby office, the immaculate man who had never done anything but fill in ledgers and count other folks' money, looked through the window at the balding lawman.

He felt that it was his duty to tell Tom Hardin about the strange change in his boss, but he was racked with guilt.

Was it disloyal to talk about Smith?

The question gnawed at the man.

Sheriff Hardin had noticed the figure casting a long shadow across his office for more than five minutes. Finally he had to rise from his comfortable chair and find out what was eating at Nash.

Hardin opened the door.

'Come on in and have a cup of coffee, Clayton.'

The sheriff had a way of inviting people to do something and making it sound like an order. Nash followed the overweight man into the stale-smelling building. The unpleasant odour of cigar smoke hung on the air inside the office.

Hardin poured a cup of coffee for the clerk and thrust it into the man's hands.

'Spit it out.'

'What?'

'Whatever's chewing at your craw. Spit it out.' The sheriff poured himself a cup of the black beverage and returned the pot to the top of the stove.

Clayton Nash sipped at the coffee and then sat down next to the cluttered desk.

'I'm not sure I should even be here, Sheriff.'

Hardin placed his ample rear on to his chair and sighed.

'Must be important, Clayton. You ain't the sort to come calling on this old lawman. Tell me what's troubling you.'

Nash held the hot cup in the palms of his hands and looked into the black liquid.

'Mr Smith had a note put under the door just after closing time. I don't know what was in it but it must have been very upsetting. When I left the bank, he was crying in his office.'

Hardin lowered his cup and looked at the man.

'Crying?'

'Yes, sir. Like a baby.'

'Tell me more.' Hardin rested his coffee-cup on his desk and looked hard at the man. He had known Jed Smith for years and could not imagine anything capable of upsetting the banker.

Nash took a deep breath and gazed up at the smoke-stained ceiling.

'He asked me to put a lamp in the bank window.'

Sheriff Hardin rubbed his whiskers. 'Have you ever been asked to put a lamp in the window before, Clayton?'

'No, sir. Never.'

Hardin opened the top drawer of his desk and produced a bottle of whiskey. He waved the bottle at Nash.

'You want some of this to take away the taste of the coffee?'

Nash nodded and held his cup out.

The sheriff poured a shot of the spirit into Nash's cup and repeated the action with his own.

'He was OK until some critter slipped the note under the bank door, you say?'

'Perfectly OK, Sheriff.'

'Then we can assume that there was something in that note that shook old Jed up real bad.' Hardin swallowed his primed coffee in one shot. 'But what?'

'I have a bad feeling about this, Sheriff,' Clayton said. He downed his own coffee in one swallow.

'Have there been any strangers in the bank?'

Nash shook his head. 'None that I can remember. Just the regulars.'

Tom Hardin rose from his chair and adjusted his gun belt.

'You did the right thing coming over and telling me about this, Clayton. Go home now and I'll try and find out what the hell's going on.'

Nash stood up and placed his empty

cup on the desk. 'Please do not tell Mr Smith that it was I who spoke with you.'

Hardin nodded. 'Don't fret none. I'll not tell him that we talked.'

Nash hurried out of the office and made his way along the boardwalk in the direction of his lodgings. The sheriff lifted his Stetson off a hatrack and placed it on his head. He closed the door behind him and stared at the bank down the street.

Something was going on in Cripple Creek and he wanted to know what it was.

'Looks like I'm gonna pay Jed Smith a visit,' Hardin told himself.

13

Hardin seated himself in the plush leather chair and looked over the magnificent desk at the uncharacteristically upset banker. He had hammered at the side door for more than five minutes with a fist that was now feeling bruised, before Jed Smith allowed his old friend in.

'Why are you here, Tom?' Smith asked, resting his elbows on the green-leather desk top.

Sheriff Hardin rubbed the side of his hand.

'I just thought that it was a while since you offered me any of that fine French brandy you hide in that bureau.'

Smith lowered his head until his brow rested on the knuckles of his hands. He remained seated.

'Help yourself, Tom. You know where it is.'

The lawman quietly got up from the chair, walked to the mahogany bureau and opened the large lower-left door. He bent down and lifted the silver-plated tray and carried the crystal-cut decanter with four matching glasses across to Smith's desk.

Tom Hardin said nothing as he removed the stopper from the neck of the decanter and poured two large measures of the aromatic brandy into the crystal-cut glasses.

Smith accepted his drink with a hand that could not stop trembling. Somehow he managed to put the glass to his dry lips and swallow a mouthful of the fiery liquid. For a moment it seemed that the fumes of the alcohol had lifted the man's spirits as he leaned back against the padded leather of his chair.

The sheriff took a sip of the brandy and then proceeded to top up both their glasses before resting his hip on the edge of the large desk.

He watched the banker the way that an eagle watches its chosen prey whilst floating on a high warm thermal. He too was waiting for an opportunity when he might find his friend composed enough to tell him what was wrong and why his face was stained with the unmistakable marks of tears.

'Sorry about your window, Jed,' Hardin said as warm brandy trickled down his throat.

'Window?' Smith had another sip of his drink.

'The one that Iron Eyes shot out this morning,' the sheriff reminded the confused banker.

Smith shrugged. 'I'd forgotten all about that. It seems like a million years ago.'

Hardin had noticed the scrap of paper tucked under the blotter near the banker's elbow. He rested his hand on the desk and tried to divert the attention of the man who seemed to be guarding it from prying eyes.

'You ought to have that old bureau checked out, Jed. Looks like there's woodworm in it.'

Smith turned his head and stared blankly at the tall bureau. He was about to speak when the lawman's hand grabbed at the note and pulled it from its hiding-place. Tom Hardin unfolded it, then read it as he moved away from the desk. Before Smith had reached his friend to retrieve the paper, Hardin had already taken in its words.

'So that's why you're spooked,' the sheriff said as Smith's shaking hands grabbed the paper from him.

Both men stood face to face in the centre of the office. For what seemed an eternity nothing was said. Then the banker's shoulders began to shake as emotion overwhelmed him once more.

Hardin grabbed his friend's shoulders and pulled him to him.

'Don't you worry, Jed. You ain't alone in this. Whoever has Rosie ain't gonna know what hit them.'

Smith walked away from the law officer, picked up his glass and downed the remainder of its contents. He shuddered, then turned his head and stared at Hardin.

'What do you mean?'

'Iron Eyes!' The sheriff said the name and smiled.

'That filthy bounty hunter? What about him?' the banker poured himself another glass of the costly spirit. 'Do you think that he's behind this? Has Iron Eyes taken my daughter?'

Tom Hardin swallowed his brandy and placed his glass on the silver tray. He toyed with the crystal decanter.

'Iron Eyes has nothing to do with kidnapping Rosie, Jed. I'd bet my pension on that. But I got me an inkling that he could track down the bastards who did, wherever they're hiding.'

For the first time since he had read the note, Smith actually felt hope creeping back into his life again.

'Would he?'

'I reckon so, Jed.'

'But why would this Iron Eyes even want to help?' Jed Smith's face suddenly began to show signs that he felt there just might be a chance of his seeing his beautiful daughter again.

'Because Iron Eyes told me that Rosie was the first gal to look at him without showing her disgust.' Hardin poured himself another brandy and swirled the liquid around in the glass thoughtfully.

Smith looked hard at the lawman. 'Doesn't he know?'

Hardin looked up into Smith's face. Their eyes met.

'Nope. He had no idea that she's blind, Jed. What stranger would? I didn't have the heart to tell him. When you look like Iron Eyes does, I reckon no female looks at you for very long. Rosie did because she could not see his scarred face.'

Smith lowered his head.

'Where is he?'

'He told me that he was headed for Sanora.' Hardin finished his brandy and headed for the office door. With his hand on its handle, he paused and turned.

'Where you going, Tom?'

'Sanora!'

14

The hideout of the ruthless Malverez and his men was a mere two miles downstream of the border-crossing along the river. A series of caves lined the tree-covered banks of the river until the fast-flowing water fell from a high cliff a hundred feet into a deep lake. The trail stopped at the top of the waterfall and only a narrow path led down to the place where the bandits hid.

The four-horse team had been left at the top of the waterfall, together with their half-dozen mounts, whilst the bandits carried their latest prize down through the undergrowth to the place that resounded with the sound of crashing water.

This was a place that had remained hidden from the eyes of most men since time had begun. Only nomadic Indians had ever set eyes upon its grandeur until the ruthless bandits had accidentally discovered it when looking for a place that offered them a safe haven from all those who hunted them.

For three years it had served its purpose well.

At the foot of the high waterfall, hidden behind the never-ending flow of cascading water, the largest of the caves lay totally obscured. This was where the bandits had stockpiled their fortune for the day when they would divide it up and finally ride off to their separate futures.

It was a day that would never come. For men such as these had long since sacrificed their futures for the gold and silver coins their past had accumulated.

There was always just one more job.

Rosie Smith was still alive when they dragged the velvet drapes from her sweat-soaked body. She lay helpless, tied like a spring calf waiting to be branded on the floor of the cave.

She would have already suffered the

same fate as so many of their other victims, would have been killed by now, if not for the fact that she had golden hair. To the hot-blooded Mexicans who were starved of female company in their remote hideout, this rare quality was the one thing that had kept Rosie Smith alive long enough to reach this unholy place.

The bandits had already mentally raped their beautiful hostage countless times before they reached the cave. Each would have done so by now if it had not been for their fear of the man who had long ago proved his ability to control them.

Malverez wanted her more than any of them.

Each of the bandits knew that he, as always, would get the first taste of this tender girl. He would be the first to take his pleasure and they would have to be satisfied with whatever scraps were left.

Malverez produced a long stiletto and cut the now-dried rawhide bonds from her wrists and ankles. Blood trickled from where the rawhide had tightened around her soft pale flesh. She could hardly move after being hogtied for so long. Gradually she managed to straighten out on the ground as every sinew in her body screamed in pain.

'We should draw lots to see who gets her first, *amigo*,' one of the bandits suggested.

'I think not, Carlos.' The bandit leader untied the blindfold and removed it from Rosie's eyes, then he pulled the gag from her mouth.

Their female hostage panted heavily as the fresh air rushed into her lungs. She remained on the ground at Malverez's feet, listening to the men walking around her. For the first time since she had been abducted, she was terrified.

'Where am I?' she gasped innocently. 'What's happening?'

'What a sweet voice,' said the bandit who answered to the name of Jose.

'Like an angel,' another added.

'It is a pity that she has to die, Malverez,' observed the bandit with the festering bullet-hole in his hand.

Malverez lifted her blonde hair and felt its softness between his fingertips. It was like the finest of silks.

They had never had such a trophy before and he knew it.

'You are right, *amigos*,' Malverez said. 'This one is very special.'

One of the other bandits moved closer to their thoughtful leader. He had never seen him so preoccupied before.

'What are you thinking?'

Malverez looked at the man and touched his cheek with the razor-sharp knife-blade.

'I am thinking that this is one female I do not want to share, *amigo*.' Malverez narrowed his eyes and stared at the five brooding men. 'I am thinking that she would make a good slave for me.'

The sound of the other men filled the

cave. They all wanted her but were now being told that she was his alone. Only killing Malverez would allow them to share this female, they all thought.

'I want her,' one of them shouted.

'We all want her,' another agreed.

Malverez listened to their voices and sat down on a wooden box filled with gold coins from previous ransoms. He lifted the knife and pointed it at his men with one hand as he stroked her hair with the other.

'Until I grow bored with her, she is mine alone, *amigos*.'

The men all ranted and raved at the seated bandit. They were angry.

'Silence, *amigos*!' Malverez ordered loudly.

For the first time since the gang of bandits had first ridden together, the other men did not listen to Malverez.

15

Train-robber Black Ben Tucker had seen many things in his long eventful life but nothing that could have prepared him for the sight of the hideous Iron Eyes. Even unconscious the infamous bounty hunter looked far more terrifying than most men when they were wide awake. Yet even though Tucker had never set eyes upon the strange scarred face of Iron Eyes before, he somehow had a feeling that he ought to recognize him.

After Iron Eyes had collapsed at the feet of the outlaw, Tucker had carried him through the cantina and into the room he had paid handsomely to rent. For such a tall man, Iron Eyes seemed to weigh very little.

Exactly why the train-robber had shown so much compassion to the man who was known throughout the West as a living ghost and a deadly killer, even Tucker could not understand. Maybe it was because Black Ben did not know who the emaciated creature he was helping was. Yet those who knew the outlaw well would have bet their last dollar against Tucker's helping anyone who required his assistance.

That was the way he was.

A man who dared to face his demons whenever they raised their heads. He assessed everyone by his own values; this had backfired several times in the past.

Iron Eyes required help, it was as simple as that. Tucker had pulled the blood-filled boot from the bounty hunter's left leg, then sent for the nearest thing that Sanora had to a real doctor.

The lay doctor had cut deeply into the gruesome wound and drained the poisonous pus from the infected area. Then the old man used everything he had inside his battered medical bag in order to save the life of Iron Eyes. For more than five hours he and Tucker battled with the delirious bounty hunter who thrashed out at the monsters who invaded his feverish mind. Five solid hours that took them into the middle of the night and beyond.

The sweat-soaked Iron Eyes screamed as the deadly venom flowed through his veins and blurred his usually keen mind. He had never ridden this trail before and there was a terror within the soul of the hunter of outlaws that chilled the two men who had willingly chosen to remain at his bedside.

These were not the screams of a normal man but the ravings of a tortured being. Neither the elderly doctor or the fugitive had ever heard anything like it.

They had held Iron Eyes down when he valiantly fought against the monsters who rose from deep down inside the depths of his soul, trying to destroy what remained of his emaciated being.

Iron Eyes had been wounded many times and lost more than his fair share of blood over the countless years since he had become a bounty hunter, but he had never before had the venom of the serpent inside him.

The elderly doctor had forced various medicinal powders down Iron Eyes' throat in an attempt to break the fever and stop the poison from destroying what was left of the incoherent man.

It was nearly midnight when the eyes of the hunter opened and he could at last see clearly again.

Iron Eyes gripped with his long thin bony fingers at the arms of the two men who were seated on either side of the cot. His chest heaved as he began to focus on the ceiling above him.

'What the hell is going on?' Iron Eyes screamed at the candlelit air and sat bolt upright.

'You OK, mister?' Black Ben Tucker asked the soaked bounty hunter.

Iron Eyes stared around the room in terror. He could not recall even reaching this place, let alone know who these two men were.

'What's happening, dammit? And who in tarnation are you varmints?'

Tucker rested a hand on the shoulder of Iron Eyes and tried to calm him down. The fever had broken but the man himself was now terrified and dangerous. The bounty hunter searched vainly for his Navy Colts and seemed terrified that his hands could not locate them.

'My guns! Where are my guns?'

'Easy, mister.' Black Ben Tucker handed the man a glass of water and watched as it was drained. He then mopped the man's wet brow as he fought to rise to his feet. 'You've been hurt real bad.'

'What?' Iron Eyes looked into the train robber's face and then at the concerned Mexican medical man. 'Hurt? I don't understand. I can't remember being hurt.'

Tucker felt as if he had a puma by the tail as he fought with the confused Iron Eyes. Finally he had to let go of the thin shoulders and watch as the weakened man rose to his feet and staggered across the small room. The exhausted bounty hunter rested his elbows on the sill of the small window and stared out at the darkness.

'It's night! How long have I been here?'

'You had a poisoned leg wound, mister,' Tucker informed Iron Eyes. 'The doc here cut out the poison and cleaned up the wound. He saved your life.'

'My work here is done, *señor*.' The doctor gathered all his instruments together and dropped them into his bag and then accepted the handful of silver coins that the train-robber forced upon him. Tucker watched as the old man left the room, then turned his attention back to the tall man who was now swaying and looking down at his leg.

'I remember now,' Iron Eyes muttered quietly. 'Damn Apache scouting party. They attacked me and I got hit by a poison arrow!'

'That explains a lot.' Tucker lit a cigar and walked to the side of the bounty hunter. He inhaled deeply and then gave the cigar to the weary man. Iron Eyes accepted it and placed it in his own mouth. He drew in as much smoke as he could and then waited for it to ease his nerves.

'I thought that I'd managed to burn the poison out,' Iron Eyes mumbled.

'Luckily you did burn some of it out,' Tucker said. 'Look what effect the remaining poison had on you. A full dose would have killed a fully grown buffalo.'

Iron Eyes savoured the smoke. 'I was in a bad way?'

'Your leg was real bad,' Tucker assured him.

'Must have been.' Iron Eyes felt the calming affect of the strong smoke and felt himself relaxing. 'Reckon I owe you, stranger. You must have saved my life.'

'Anything for a fellow gringo.' Tucker smiled broadly. 'There ain't many of us down here in ol' Mexico.'

Iron Eyes nodded and returned the cigar to Tucker.

'I can't remember much. I keep seeing a girl with long yellow hair but I'm damned if I know why. Must have been a dream.'

'Must have been the poison.' Tucker inhaled on the cigar again and then leaned his back against the wall and looked at the cold eyes of the shaking man. 'I thought you was a goner. I've never seen anyone that far gone who managed to live.'

'I recall that there are folks who say that I'm too evil to die.' Iron Eyes pushed himself away from the window and limped back to the cot. He sat down and ran his fingers through his long wet hair. 'What's your name?'

'They call me Black Ben Tucker.'

Iron Eyes shrugged. The name meant nothing to him. 'Guess I owe you my life, Black Ben Tucker.'

Black Ben smiled through the smoke that drifted from his teeth. 'You'd have done the same for me, I reckon. What's your name, mister?'

'Iron Eyes,' came the reply.

Tucker's expression altered. He had heard of this man and knew that he was reputed to kill without pity. This was the bounty hunter who was feared throughout the West. A man whom no outlaw wanted to be within a hundred miles of.

'How come you're down here in Mexico?'

Iron Eyes exhaled heavily. 'I was hunting something or someone, mister.'

'Who?' Tucker sucked on the tip of the cigar and watched the face of the seated bounty hunter.

The fog that filled his mind suddenly cleared and Iron Eyes looked up at the outlaw above him.

'You!' he replied quietly. 'It was you!

★   ★   ★

'If I had my guns, you'd be dead by now, Black Ben.' Iron Eyes growled at the train-robber who stood over him.

Tucker lowered his chin until it rested on his shirt. 'Do you always kill men who save your life, Iron Eyes?'

'I kill men who are wanted dead or alive.'

'You ain't answered my question.' Tucker paced slowly around the room with Iron Eyes' gaze tracking his every step. 'Is it your custom to kill men who've saved your life?'

The bounty hunter's gaze flashed around the room as if he were trying to find an answer to the direct question: a question that he did not have an answer for. At least not one that satisfied himself.

'You're a mighty odd character, Iron Eyes.' Tucker paused at the small dresser and opened the top drawer.

'Because I hunt vermin?'

'Nope. Because you can't seem to recognize a friend when you meet one.' Black Ben Tucker fumbled in the drawer and pulled out the pair of matched Navy Colts. He turned and faced the hunter and then tossed the guns on to the bed next to him. It was the biggest gamble Tucker had ever taken, and one he prayed he would not regret.

Iron Eyes stared at his weapons. He picked up one and checked it. It was loaded.

'You loco or something, Black Ben?'

The train-robber exhaled a long line of smoke. 'I must be, Iron Eyes. To give a pair of loaded .36s to a man who says that he's here to kill me, sounds darn crazy.'

Iron Eyes cocked the hammer of the pistol and aimed it at the smiling man. The train-robber swallowed hard and walked slowly to the open doorway.

'I'm gonna get some vittles. You want some, Iron Eyes?'

Iron Eyes lowered the lethal weapon and released its hammer before placing it back on the bed. For a reason that he could not fully comprehend, he had no desire to kill this man, however much bounty there was on his head.

'I could eat a bowl of that chilli that's stinking up the place, right about now, Black Ben.'

'Two bowls of chilli coming up.' Tucker walked out into the cantina and headed for the cooking range. He removed the cigar from his mouth and stared at his hand. It was shaking.

16

Tom Hardin drove his horse through the night at a speed he had never managed to achieve before. He checked outside Jed Smith's home before setting out for the border and the country that lay beyond. The sheriff had noticed the deep tracks of the wagon that had been used by the bandits. He had noted that the wagon tracks went south along the trail which led to Mexico. Only the coming of night had obscured the tracks as he had thundered across the wide shallow river.

Hardin had not come this way for more than five years but knew exactly the fastest route to the isolated town of Sanora. The lawman spurred his mount on and used the moon above him as his guide.

For a man who had become almost

as broad in the beam as his horse over the years of sitting behind a desk shuffling papers, Hardin rode with a skill not found in many younger men.

Forcing the faithful sorrel onward with all his strength, he cleared a sandy rise and then hauled the reins to his chest. The whitewashed buildings stood out in the moonlight below him like the teeth of a giant.

He had made it.

He dismounted, filled his hat with water from his canteen, and allowed the horse to drink as he checked his old Colt .45. It was fully loaded and greased.

When the horse had finished the last drop of the precious liquid, Hardin scooped up the Stetson and placed it back on his head. The droplets of water on his balding scalp felt good as he stepped back into the stirrup and hauled his bulk back on to the saddle.

The sheriff of Cripple Creek urged the sorrel down the sand-covered incline and rode directly at the white buildings with renewed vigour.

With every stride that the robust horse took across the soft, sandy terrain, the law officer wondered whether the bounty hunter would still be in Sanora. He had a fear that, just as after his cold-blooded dispatch of outlaw Ben Drake back at Cripple Creek, Iron Eyes might have headed off in search of his next victim.

Then as the sorrel entered the maze of white buildings and the sound of the Mexican townspeople enjoying the slightly cooler temperature that darkness always brought filled the air, he spotted the dapple-grey horse tied up outside a cantina.

Tom Hardin slowed the horse to a walk as he approached the busy building.

Light cascaded out into the street as he slowly got off his mount and gathered up the long reins. He rubbed the dust from his face and tied the sorrel to the hitching pole next to Iron Eyes' grey.

A hundred thoughts went through the mind of the sheriff as he pushed the beaded curtains apart and stared into the busy cantina.

Would Iron Eyes help him find Rosie Smith?

What if he had continued to drink whiskey at the same rate as he had done in Cripple Creek and was now lying in a drunken stupor?

A few steps inside the cantina answered most of the questions that had burned their way into the mind of the sheriff during the hours that he had spent in the saddle riding here.

The unmistakable figure of Iron Eyes was sitting next to Black Ben Tucker at a filthy table with a bowl of half-eaten chilli before him.

Iron Eyes looked even paler than when Hardin had last seen him. There were corpses buried in Boot Hill that looked more alive than the bounty hunter.

Tom Hardin removed his hat and made his way through the cantina's customers until he reached the table and then stared down at Iron Eyes. He spotted the left leg which was covered in iodine and crude catgut stitches.

'What the hell happened to you, son?' the sheriff asked in a tone that displayed his utter shock at the sight before him.

Tucker looked at the sheriff and focused on the star. He felt uneasy once more.

'Iron Eyes got himself into a little trouble with a bunch of Apache's, Sheriff.'

'Black Ben Tucker?' Hardin said the name he had read on the Wanted poster so many times.

'Sit down, Sheriff,' Iron eyes said bluntly. 'Join me and my friend in a little supper.'

Hardin's mouth fell open.

'Your friend? I thought you was hunting this man's bounty, Iron Eyes.'

Iron Eyes glanced at the train-robber and then back at the sheriff. A smile crawled over his thin cracked lips.

17

The sound of the water as it fell unceasingly into the deep lake outside the mouth of the large cave filled the ears of all the bandits. Normally it would have helped them fall asleep, but not on this night.

This night it was different.

Malverez had never been so close to what could only be described as a mutiny before. For a decade he had controlled his followers and they had obeyed his every order because they knew that his was a brain that calculated everything methodically and without any hint of emotion.

He had made them a fortune but this night there was something the bandits valued far more than the wooden chests filled with gold and silver coins.

The bandit leader had been lying beside the silent Rosie Smith for hours and yet he had done nothing. The eyes of the five other bandits had not closed since he had made his dramatic announcement. The lighted torches illuminated every one of the cold eyes that were trained on him.

The bandits were waiting. Waiting for their chance.

They wanted her and Malverez had not dared to take his own selfish pleasures for fear of turning his back on the men whom he knew were quite as ruthless as he was himself.

Malverez knew that a knife or bullet would find his back as soon as he showed it to them. The bandit leader was troubled. These were five angry men who faced him. He propped his head against the huge rolled up blankets and knew that any one of them was more than capable of killing him without a second thought.

Malverez lit yet another cigar and drew the putrid smoke into his lungs. For the last hour he had felt more and more uneasy as the bandits seemed to edge ever closer.

It was the middle of the night and yet none of them was willing to succumb to the tiredness that had threatened to overwhelm them hours earlier.

The leader of the bandits dragged his pistols from their holsters and sucked on the long cigar. He laid the guns on his chest and watched the eyes that flashed in the flickering torchlight before him.

Would they actually attack him?

Malverez knew that no amount of the free tequila he had plied them with could calm this storm. It had gone too far. There was only one way that he might stop them now, and that was to give them what they so desperately wanted.

He could give them the girl and it would be over.

There was one other choice open to him though. Malverez knew that he could still keep the beautiful prize for himself if he pretended that he was willing to let them have her.

But he would then have to kill them all when they started to take their pleasure.

It was a risky course of action to take and would probably end in disaster for all of them, he thought. Malverez wanted this female more than any other he had ever taken by force. She seemed different from all the rest who lay buried beneath the sands of Mexico.

He knew that he would have to fight for her.

The five men had ridden with him for ten long years and yet he knew that only fear had ever kept them in check. There was no loyalty in their ranks. Just the fear of the weak when faced with the mighty.

Now they loomed like vultures waiting for him to sleep. There was no way that he would ever awaken from that sleep if he did not do something to calm them down.

Malverez touched the hair of the female beside him and gritted what was left of his teeth. She did not move a muscle. The bandit did not know whether she was asleep or just frozen with fear. He glared at the men through the smoke of his cigar, then picked up the two matching pistols and rose to his feet.

The five other bandits all stood up with their hands on the grips of their own guns and faced him defiantly. Whatever he had decided to do, they could only guess at.

Malverez flicked the ash off his cigar with the barrel of one of his pistols and then began to laugh.

He had made up his mind.

He would try and bluff them into doing nothing with the promise of their getting what they wanted.

'We have had a very eventful day, *amigos*,' Malverez joked as he slipped one gun back into its holster and twirled the other on his index finger.

'We want to share this female with you,' Carlos grunted angrily.

'And you shall.'

The five bandits' faces went blank.

He had confused them, if only briefly. They stared at him as he removed his sombrero and spun it across the cave.

'You have changed your mind about keeping her for yourself?'

Malverez rubbed the cold gun barrel over his unshaven cheek and smiled broadly.

'I was lying when I said that I would keep this girl for my own satisfaction, Jose.'

The bandit stepped forward and tilted his head at the seemingly jovial Malverez.

'It was a bad joke, *amigo*,' one of the others commented.

'*Sí*, it was a very bad joke. But when you all lost your tempers, I got angry. I should have said something a long time ago but the tequila made me stupid.'

'So we can have her?' Jose asked, rubbing his groin with his pistol.

Malverez nodded.

'You can all have your way with her until she dies of happiness or exhaustion, *amigo*. But after I have tasted her first.'

The eager bandits all nodded as one. 'When?'

Malverez was trying to buy himself time.

'Tomorrow. We are all too tired to fully enjoy ourselves tonight.'

Carlos holstered his gun first.

'This is why Malverez is such a great leader, *amigos*.'

The bandit leader nodded, holstered his pistol and watched the men moving to their bedrolls. He had bought himself a little time but how much and what it would cost, was yet to be resolved.

Malverez moved back to his own bedroll and stared down at the hair of Rosie Smith flowing from beneath the velvet drape she had used as a blanket.

He swallowed hard.

18

Iron Eyes sat on the cot and dragged the still blood-soaked mule-ear boot back on to his wounded leg. If he was in pain, he hid it well from his two companions.

'This is plumb loco, Iron Eyes,' Black Ben Tucker said loud enough for the entire town of Sanora to hear.

'Reckon so,' Iron Eyes agreed, picking up his pair of Navy Colts and tucking them into his belt. He ran the palms of his hands over the well-used grips and sighed heavily. 'It's time for me to do what I do best.'

'You ain't strong enough,' Black Ben Tucker said, frowning.

Sheriff Hardin touched the sleeve of the train-robber and made a face that told the younger man to calm down.

'Ease up, son. Iron Eyes knows what he's doing.'

'But this man has just recovered from having poison dug out of his leg, Sheriff,' Tucker protested. 'He ain't in no fit state to do nothing, let alone ride.'

'I'm OK!' Iron Eyes insisted, reaching for a bottle of whiskey on the cot and taking a long swallow.

'You're as weak as a kitten, Iron Eyes,' Tucker insisted.

Hardin nodded.

'He knows that, Tucker.'

'Then why ask him for help?' Black Ben asked.

'Because the life of a young girl is at stake. I know of only one man who can possibly track down the bastards who took her. One man who has the skill to kill anything that's capable of raising guns in anger. That one man is Iron Eyes. Rosie Smith has just one chance in hell of being saved.'

Black Ben rubbed his face in frustration. 'It'll kill him, Sheriff. He's spent most of the night racked with fever.'

Iron Eyes stood up and pressed his left leg down hard on to floor as if trying to gauge the pain level he would have to withstand.

'I'll find her, boys,' he said, adjusting the grips of his guns, which jutted from his belt.

'We ain't got much time left,' Hardin said anxiously. 'I figure whoever abducted Rosie has no intention of keeping their side of the bargain and returning her after they get the ransom money from Smith.'

'I want to ride with you, Iron Eyes,' Black Ben said to the pale bounty hunter. 'I want to help you find this girl.'

Iron Eyes nodded. 'Fine.'

'I'm pretty good with this old Colt, boys,' Hardin said, slapping the holster on his hip.

Iron Eyes attached his spurs to his boots and then walked from the room, across the cantina and out into the street. Tucker and Hardin followed the tall limping bounty hunter like chicks trailing a mother hen. Iron Eyes stood and listened to the sounds of guitars and trumpets echoing all around him. Sanora was noisy with the Mexicans who had slept throughout the baking-hot afternoon.

'If Smith pays them, they'll not get a chance to spend that money, Sheriff.'

Sheriff Hardin and Black Ben Tucker squared up to the brooding man who was checking his saddle.

'What do you mean, son?' the sheriff asked.

''Coz they'll all be dead as soon as I catch up with them,' came the grim reply.

★   ★   ★

The three riders had made remarkable progress through what remained of the night to reach the banks of the river. Like a man wearing a death mask, Iron Eyes sat astride his dapple-grey staring at the moonlit ground as the water lashed at the hoofs of their horses.

He had somehow worked out exactly how many riders had crossed the border since he had ridden through the shallow water so many hours earlier.

Iron Eyes pulled his left boot from the stirrup and then raised his right leg over the neck of the drinking grey. He slid off his saddle, taking the full impact of the ground with his good leg.

The eyes of the bounty hunter seemed to notice things in the dark mud that neither of his companions could see. The honed skill of the hunter were now coming into play. He could track anything and it showed.

'My tracks are over there.' Iron Eyes pointed behind them. 'I can see your horse's hoofprints a few feet nearer, Sheriff. Then we have the grooves of a wagon that turned and headed down river. Five other riders cut through here between your sorrel and the wagon. They headed on after the wagon.'

Tucker dismounted and held the reins to his magnificent black horse in his gloved hands. He walked to the side of the tall grim-faced man and rested a hand on the broad shoulder.

'I'm impressed.'

Iron Eyes did not seem to care what either of the men thought about his skill as a tracker. All that filled his mind was the fact that the girl that he had met back in Cripple Creek was probably in more danger than even he could imagine. He had seen what men could do to innocent females many times and it turned his guts.

'We have to head down there.' The bounty hunter aimed his thin index finger in the direction in which the shallow river was flowing.

Black Ben Tucker pulled up the collar of his coat and tried to stop the cool breeze from chilling his neck.

'Me and Hardin can take it from here, Iron Eyes,' Tucker said softly. 'They must be holed up darn close.'

Iron Eyes glared at the man's face. Even in the light of the moon his anger could be easily seen. 'I'm not quitting, Black Ben. Without me you two fools would never find the girl or the men who have her.'

Sheriff Hardin steered his mount alongside the two men and stared down at them.

'How far do you reckon we have to go?'

'Not far. A few miles at most.' Iron Eyes grabbed the reins of his grey and pulled it around. He held on to the saddle horn and threw himself up on to the back of the nervous animal.

Tucker stepped into his stirrup and mounted the black horse.

'How can you be so damn certain?'

Iron Eyes pulled his bottle of whiskey from one of the satchels behind his saddle cantle and removed its cork. He swallowed two massive shots of the fiery liquid, and then replaced the cork and dropped the bottle back into the bag behind him.

''Coz I can smell the vermin, Black Ben!'

Tucker stared in disbelief at the bounty hunter, who was urging his mount to start walking along the tracks of his prey.

'You can smell them? Are you joshing me?'

Iron Eyes sniffed at the night air. 'Cougars leave a scent that a hunter can smell a mile off. All critters have their own stink. Rosie Smith had perfume on; I can smell that too. I can smell the bastards who rode down here with her, and I'll know them when we meet up.'

'And then?' the sheriff asked the gaunt rider as he drew his horse level.

'When my nostrils are filled with their scent, I'll kill the whole lot of them,' Iron Eyes replied. His eyes were studying the wet ground as he forced his dapple-grey on and on.

'You forget there are three of us, Iron Eyes,' the train-robber added.

'I don't need either of you. When I start killing just stay behind my gun barrels.' Iron Eyes tapped his spurs into the flesh of his horse and sat bolt upright as the animal increased its pace.

19

The morning sun had risen and traced its way across the deep lake at the foot of the cascade until its golden rays penetrated the ever-moving curtain of shimmering water. Within the cave the light of the new day spread quickly over the seven silent recumbent souls, yet two of their number had not closed their eyes.

Malverez still lay with his hand on the handle of one of his prized Colts, watching the five other bandits who continued to snore.

Rosie Smith lay beneath the heavy velvet drapes pretending to be asleep. She had not moved for nearly six hours for fear of arousing her abductors and making them complete the job they had already started.

She knew that it must already be dawn. The sound of singing birds had alerted her to the beginning of the new day many minutes earlier.

The warmth of the sun had filtered through the never-ceasing curtain of water, falling from the hundred-foot-high cliff in front of the cave entrance.

The gentle heat touched Rosie's exposed cheek and she felt even more afraid than she had done since the ruthless bandits had taken her by force from her home.

For her entire life she had wondered what being able to see might be like. But Rosie had nothing to compare her blindness with as she had never had the gift of sight. To her the world was filled with the aromas of things and people. Sounds came from everywhere and she had learned to evaluate them as only those denied a vital sense can. Touch had also been another of her senses which meant more to her than those who had vision to assist their journey through life.

Lying beneath the makeshift blanket, Rosie found herself wishing that she could actually see her enemies, even if it were for only a fleeting moment.

The sleeping bandits were all around her and their snores gave her some idea as to their whereabouts but the crashing noise of the waterfall made everything else confused.

She knew that to escape the clutches of these men, she had to be able to see. It was obvious to the intelligent female that she had been carried down a steep slope and brought into a cave and that it was behind a waterfall. She knew it was impossible for her to negotiate the return route to the top of the trail where the men had left their horses and the wagon.

Rosie felt the hand of Malverez on her shoulder for the umpteenth time and felt her entire being go rigid. She had not been able to understand a single word that the Mexican bandits had been saying to each other during the night, but she knew they were heated.

She had little if no knowledge of life,

and had been protected from all who might have shown any interest in her, but she felt that these men wanted something from her that she was unwilling to give.

The strong hand of the bandit leader pulled her shoulder until she felt herself rolling over to face him. Her heart began to thunder inside her chest.

What did he want? her mind cried out.

'Do not make a sound, my pretty one,' Malverez whispered into her ear.

* * *

Sheriff Tom Hardin had a big decision to make. It was probably the biggest one of his entire life. Should he tell Iron Eyes that the girl who had not turned away from his ghastly scarred features had only not done so because she was blind? Her beautiful pale blue eyes simply could not see the hideous vision that made all others shun him.

Or should he allow the injured

bounty hunter to continue under the delusion that Rosie Smith actually liked what she had seen when she looked at him?

With a man as unpredictable as Iron Eyes, either choice might have devastating, if not lethal, consequences. The sheriff knew that the bounty hunter was not a man to mess with, even when he was fit. But he was far from fit. He was like a wounded animal as he silently steered the grey mount.

What effect would the truth have on him? Hardin did not want to take the risk of finding out but he knew that he would soon have somehow to inform Iron Eyes that the girl they were seeking was actually totally blind. To fail to do so would put Rosie Smith in even more danger.

But if Iron Eyes knew that the female he was attempting to rescue was actually blind, would he continue?

Could Sheriff Hardin and Black Ben Tucker find her without the undoubted tracking skills of Iron Eyes? It seemed doubtful as neither man had any experience at tracking anything, let alone cold-blooded bandits.

Hardin knew it was cruel to allow the sick bounty hunter to remain ignorant of the truth, but he was afraid.

Iron Eyes wanted to find the lovely Rosie Smith and there was nothing that could stop him from doing so. He was like a stick of dynamite with its fuse already lit.

Tom Hardin knew that he had to tell the grim rider the truth soon, but not quite yet. The sheriff had to wait until they reached their destination and pray that the bounty hunter would not turn on him instead of the men who had kidnapped the innocent Rosie.

The two horsemen followed the dapple-grey mount as its master guided it away from the river's edge and into thick lush undergrowth.

Iron Eyes raised his arm and stopped his horse.

His two companions reined in their own horses to either side of the grey and stared at the seemingly impenetrable mass of trees and brush before them.

'What's wrong, son?' asked the sheriff.

Iron Eyes' head turned, he looked at the older man. There was no expression on the face that looked as if it were carved from stone. He reached out and touched the mouth of the lawman and then threw his right leg over the neck of the dapple-grey and slid silently to the ground.

Hardin glanced at Tucker and both men dismounted as quietly as they could. They knew that the tall hunter had either seen or heard something that they were not skilled enough to spot.

Iron Eyes tied his reins tightly to a tree-branch and indicated to the two men to copy him.

They did.

'When the shooting starts, I don't want our horses to hightail it out of here,' the bounty hunter said in a low voice. 'We're a long way from the nearest livery stable and I ain't gonna walk far on this leg.'

Black Ben moved to the side of the limping Iron Eyes.

'What have you seen?'

Iron Eyes touched the side of his nose. His nostrils were flared. 'I ain't seen nothing. But I can sure smell something.'

'Smell what?'

'Horses. Maybe a dozen of the critters.' Iron Eyes began limping through the tall grass; even handicapped by his injured leg, he still managed to walk without any sound.

Sheriff Hardin and Black Ben Tucker followed the man in the long trail-coat through the brush, which was taller than any of them. They could hear the sound of loose bullets rolling around against each other inside the deep pockets.

'Where we headed?' Hardin asked quietly.

Iron Eyes did not reply.

'What's that strange noise, Iron

136

Eyes?' Black Ben asked as the sound of water crashing into a lake filled the air all around them.

'Waterfall,' Iron Eyes said bluntly.

He had no idea where his nose was leading them but knew that the bandits' horses were somewhere up ahead of them. The question was, were their masters also there? If they were, would they be expecting anyone to be tracking them? So many questions ran through the mind of the bounty hunter. None of them had any answer.

The three men walked for a quarter of a mile with the sound of the waterfall getting louder with every stride. Suddenly, Iron Eyes stopped walking and the two men almost bumped into his back.

'Look!'

Black Ben rubbed his chin and stared at the clearing. The sight of the wagon and its team of four horses still in their traces made him reach for his guns.

Iron Eyes moved silently to their left, and pulled a leafy branch aside and held it down for his two followers to look at the six tethered horses a mere ten feet from the wagon.

'They must be damn close, Iron Eyes,' Black Ben said, raising his guns as if expecting to have the bandits jump out at them from a secret hiding-place at any time.

The bounty hunter allowed the branch to return to its place and then stared down at the pair of pistols in the hands of the train robber.

'Holster them irons, Black Ben,' he ordered.

'But them *hombres* must be close,' Tucker said nervously. His eyes flashed at every leaf that surrounded them.

'They ain't here.' Iron Eyes limped past the horses with his two skittish followers on his heels.

'They must be. They couldn't have gotten out of here without their horses, son,' the sheriff commented.

Iron Eyes continued through the dense undergrowth. It seemed that he did not feel the cruel thorns that ripped

138

at his flesh as he forced a path where none had existed before.

Iron Eyes stood on the very edge of the sheer drop and stared coldly at the waterfall and the lake below them.

'They're down there!'

20

Rosie Smith had wondered what the bowels of hell must be really like a thousand times over the years of being taken to church every Sunday morning. She had listened to the minister rant and rave from his pulpit and noticed more than most that he hammered his fist down on to the pages of the Good Book at the end of the every warning.

She had long since lost faith in his words and had used those services to drift into her own black world where there was no colour to distract her. Long ago she had realized that the minister did not preach about loving God but used his position to make people fear the Almighty.

It appeared that everything was bathed in sin. Yet she had no knowledge of what sin actually was. For her entire short life she had wondered about that.

What was sin?

As Malverez had turned her over to face him and the stench of his breath almost made her vomit, she suddenly began to realize the true meaning of the word.

The bandit leader had peeled the drape from her and used it to cover them both. The razor-sharp blade of his stiletto had touched her throat and she had taken this as a warning not to open her mouth and make a sound.

The roughness of his whiskers as they scraped the flesh of her soft neck filled her with fear. She had prayed to be given the gift of sight during the night in order that she might be able to escape but now as his lips sucked at her skin, she was thankful that she could not see the monster who held her tightly.

The knife blade had cut the bodice of her dress-top and he had scooped her firm breasts in his greasy hands. He sucked her nipples until they became erect and then grunted like an animal beneath the cover of the velvet drape.

Rosie shuddered with his every movement. Was this the sin that the minister had been so obsessed with for so many years? If so, then it was none of her doing.

Yet would the good churchgoing people of Cripple Creek take that into consideration when branding her with the deeds of this creature?

It seemed that there was no part of her body that the man's lips, tongue and teeth did not want to explore. She could feel the pain of the bruises his powerful hands were creating as they forced her to remain exactly where he wanted her. She did not need sight to know that the top of her dress had been removed. Her ears had heard the tearing and her skin felt the cold air tracing over it.

She was half naked.

Was this a sin?

Even the knowledge of the deadly knife no longer gave her cause to be fearful as she squirmed, trying desperately to get away from the man who was all over her. But there was no escaping his hands and mouth. Malverez had done this many times to many other captive females and she had never even been kissed before.

Then she felt one of his hands beneath the curve of her spine as he lifted her off the ground. His fingers grabbed at her knee and moved along her thigh at a speed that she had never thought possible. A sensation raced through her but she could not understand why.

Was this excitement?

She tried to force him away but his strength seemed to have no limits. She was totally under his control.

Suddenly Rosie gasped. His fingers were crawling inside her undergarments like worms. She began to realize what his ultimate goal must be.

Only the sharp tip of the knife at her throat prevented her from screaming out.

★   ★   ★

The three men stared down into the lake and the white spray that rose from the water that crashed continuously from the hundred-foot-high cliff. Shafts of light arched like a splintered rainbow over the humid scene. This was not a place in which any of them felt at ease. A massive tree-trunk was balanced over the precipice at the top of the falls. Iron Eyes studied it carefully with interest. Its branches were full of well-nourished leaves and that told the experienced hunter that the roots of the fallen tree must still be buried deep into the ground anchoring it high above the steep drop.

From where the three men stood it was a perilous journey down to the foot of the waterfall. Iron Eyes knew that there had to be another trail, otherwise the men could not have managed to get Rosie Smith or themselves down there. And he knew that they were down there, he could smell the stench of their crawling hides filling his nostrils.

The bounty hunter knew that she

was there too. Even after so many hours, her perfume still lingered on the air for one capable of sensing it.

'Are you sure that they're down there?' Black Ben asked as he felt the hairs beneath his black bandanna rise.

'Yep. They're all down there OK.' Iron Eyes pointed a bony finger. 'I figure they must be behind that waterfall.'

'Impossible!' Hardin heard himself say.

'There's a cave there,' Iron Eyes insisted. 'Look at the way the sunlight is reflecting off that water. There has to be a cave there.'

Tucker moved to the side of the taller man and swallowed hard as he looked down at the drop. 'There ain't no way of even getting down there from here. They must be holed up around here someplace.'

'I sure can't see no trail leading down there, Iron Eyes,' Tom Hardin added.

'There is one and I'll find it with or without you.' Iron Eyes pulled out a cigar from inside one of his deep jacket pockets and placed it between his teeth. He struck a match with his thumbnail, cupped the flame to the tip of his cigar and inhaled.

Black Ben stared at the face of the tall man. Its pale chiselled features showed the strain that the last twenty-four hours had racked on the pitifully lean frame.

'I ain't hankering to break my neck trying to get down there, Iron Eyes.'

'Then stay here like a couple of old women. I'm headin' on down.' The bounty hunter moved to his left and forced his way through the brush. Nervously, the two other men followed him even though they were less than a couple of feet from the edge of the sheer drop.

After twenty yards Iron Eyes stopped and stared at the ground at his feet. He pointed and his two companions bent over to study the tracks he had just discovered.

'Boot-prints,' Tucker gasped.

'Boot-prints heading toward the edge of the cliff.' Hardin sighed heavily.

Iron Eyes looked at Tucker.

'Go and get me a saddle rope off one of them horses back there, Black Ben.'

The train-robber raised an eyebrow. 'Saddle rope?'

'Yep!' Iron Eyes watched as the handsome outlaw obediently turned and headed off through the under-growth towards the horses that they had passed a score of yards behind them.

Sheriff Hardin knew that he had now to come clean with the obviously weary bounty hunter. He had to tell him the truth. 'This is gonna be tough for me to say, son. But I've got to tell you before you . . .'

Iron Eyes looked down at the sweating face before him and moved to the man's side. 'You got a secret?'

'It's about Rosie,' Hardin mumbled.

'She's blind,' Iron Eyes announced. He turned his head to look at Black Ben returning with the long coiled cutting rope over his shoulder.

The lawman gulped. 'You knew?'

'Yeah, I knew.' Iron Eyes' voice faded into silence.

Black Ben Tucker reached the two men and handed the rope to Iron Eyes.

'What's wrong?'

'Nothing's wrong, Black Ben.' Iron Eyes began to unwind the rope as he walked in the tracks of the bandits. 'Hardin seemed to think that I'd not figure out that only a blind girl could look me in the face. I knew she couldn't see with them beautiful eyes of hers. Maybe I just liked the idea that I was wrong.'

'To rescue a blind girl might prove a tad difficult,' Tucker observed.

'She's worth it,' Iron Eyes said over his shoulder.

The sheriff and the train-robber followed the tall figure through the dense brush towards the very top of the high waterfall. Without any hint of fear for his own safety, Iron Eyes stepped to the edge of the cliff-top and stared at the narrow trail which wound its way down to the foot of the waterfall.

'Why do you want the cutting rope, Iron Eyes?' Tucker asked the injured man, who continued to unwind the long rope as he limped towards the fallen tree which jutted out a good twenty feet past the top of the waterfall.

Iron Eyes made a lasso and tossed it over the largest of the stocky branches, then tightened it.

'I got me an idea.'

Neither man liked the sound of Iron Eyes' reply. It hinted at his doing something that bordered on the suicidal.

'Hold on there, son,' the sheriff said, moving to the hunter's side. 'What you figurin' on doing?'

Tucker removed his hat and dried his brow on his black sleeve.

'He's figuring on using that rope to lower himself down to the floor of the waterfall, Sheriff.'

The cold eyes flashed at Tucker and then to Hardin. Iron Eyes said nothing as he pulled at the rope knot until he

149

was convinced that the branch would take his weight.

Sheriff Hardin raised his hands in the air.

'Are you loco? You ain't strong enough to climb down that rope, son. It must be a fifty- or sixty-foot drop.'

Iron Eyes wrapped the end of the rope around his waist and tied a knot.

'Nearer to a hundred foot by my reckoning, Sheriff. But I ain't gonna walk down that track on this leg.' Iron Eyes corrected the older man as he stepped up on to the broad trunk of the tree and checked his balance. Sweat was dripping like water from the strands of limp hair that hung over his face. He was in agony but refused to let either of the men who had tagged along with him know.

To them, as to every other person who had ever encountered Iron Eyes, he had to give the appearance of being invincible. To show any sign of weakness was simply not in his nature.

The bounty hunter lifted the yards of

slack rope up in his bony hands and then started to make his way tentatively along the tree-trunk.

The poison that had tortured him throughout the previous night still haunted Iron Eyes. His head kept filling with the remnants of the venomous fog but somehow he managed to shake it off.

'Are you OK?' Black Ben shouted out over the noise of the rumbling waterfall. 'You look like death itself.'

'Thank you kindly, Black Ben. I just hope this rope is long enough. I'd hate to end up dangling half-way down,' Iron Eyes said, looking at how much slack rope he had and trying to judge how far it was to the bottom of the wet cliff.

'You better pray that it ain't too long,' Sheriff Hardin called out.

Iron Eyes shrugged and took another step.

'I hadn't thought about that, old man. Could be real messy if'n it is.'

Hardin and Tucker watched in total

awe as Iron Eyes limped towards the end of the fallen tree. He was already past the point of no return when he turned and looked at his companions.

'You two had better make your way down the trail and get them hammers cocked ready for action.' Iron Eyes stared into the rising spray that obscured everything below the prostrate tree. 'Because I'm gonna jump in about two minutes time. I'd hate to get there before you do.'

The two men turned and rushed through the tall grass at the top of the cliff. Carefully they scrambled down the steep trail with their guns in their hands.

They knew that they had to reach the foot of the waterfall and see if their companion was right about there being a cave behind it.

The narrow trail was damp with the morning dew that the slowly rising sun had yet to find and dry. They slid and staggered on their way down the twisting trail.

At last they reached the banks of the lake and stared at the wet rocks which rose up behind the falling water.

Black Ben Tucker tapped the sheriff's arm and pointed behind the white cascading spray. They could just make out the black outline of a cave set back behind the crashing waterfall.

'Iron Eyes was right. There is a damn cave.'

Their weaponry was cocked just as Iron Eyes had ordered.

21

Most men would have been afraid. But Iron Eyes was unlike most men. He defied death because it had been his constant companion since he had first felt its cruel hand resting on his broad bony shoulders. Inhaling deeply on the remants of his cigar, Iron Eyes held firmly on to the rope with his left hand and to one of his cocked Navy Colts with the other. He edged closer to the end of the tree. His cold eyes gazed down at the lake far below him and at his two companions. They were in position and ready.

Now it was his turn.

He tossed the cigar away and watch it disappear beneath his high vantage point. With smoke trailing from his teeth, the bounty hunter leapt off the massive tree and out into the air. Iron Eyes hurtled down through the misty spray of the waterfall far faster than he had imagined possible.

Yet he still felt nothing.

The rocky ground at the edge of the falls seemed to be coming up at him at a speed he had not anticipated. Iron Eyes gripped on to the rope as tightly as he could and wondered whether the old sheriff might have been right.

What if the rope was too long?

If so, he would crash into the rocks at the side of the lake with such force, it would break every bone in his body. Yet still he was not afraid.

Only someone who savoured life itself feared losing it.

Suddenly Iron Eyes heard the rope starting to buzz above him and knew that it had reached its full length. It went taut and began to whiplash his entire body. Iron Eyes raised his legs in the air as the rope began to vibrate violently as he swung over the heads of Tucker and Hardin. Then he hurtled back into the air once more.

The bounty hunter screwed his eyes

up and stared at the slack in the rope above him. He was falling again at an incredible speed down towards his two companions. He was like a helpless rag-doll, desperately trying to regain control of the rope in his hand.

Then he bounced heavenward again. It felt as if every bone in his body had been stretched to twice its length. Iron Eyes hung on tightly to the rope as his body was thrown around in the air, again whipping him like a human slingshot.

Iron Eyes found himself swinging down towards the wall of water. He was convinced that there was a cave hidden behind it.

This time he was on target.

Forcing his feet together, Iron Eyes used every ounce of his dwindling strength to control the wet saddle rope and to make himself aim straight into the thundering cascade.

It was like hitting a brick wall as Iron Eyes' entire body forced its way straight through the water spray at the centre of the falls.

Iron Eyes knew that if he was wrong about there being a cave there, he would crash into a solid rockface, but there was no time now to worry about trivial things like death.

He had made his choice and there was nothing left to do but see it through to the bitter end. He was committed and convinced that he was right.

His flared nostrils could still smell the stench of the bandits and the sweet perfume of the female. They were there all right.

As Iron Eyes' feet hurtled through the water he released his grip on the rope with his left hand and tugged at the slip knot around his waist. He felt the rope give way, then his thin body was free and flying feet first into the cave.

He held on to the grip of his pistol with one hand and rubbed the water from his eyes with the other. Iron Eyes felt his boots hit the floor of the cave and an agonizing pain ripped through him. He went head over heels, crashing heavily into the sleeping bandits.

Tossing his bedraggled long hair off his face he gritted his teeth and stared around the cave quickly. He had only a split second to figure out where he was and where each of his enemies was.

Iron Eyes fired one shot into the roof of the cave and then felt himself being hauled at by the men all around him. Arms grabbed at his legs and he instinctively fired point blank into the stunned bandit's head. Blood splattered all over the tall gaunt figure as he kicked out at the lifeless body.

The four other men scrambled to their feet. Iron Eyes could see the flashing gun metal of the pistols around him. He thrashed out with the barrel of his Navy Colt. The bandits were all around him when he spotted Malverez rising from the side of the half-naked Rosie Smith.

Iron Eyes felt his temper rising beyond the point where most men could have coped. He tried to aim at the bandit leader but felt his frail body being knocked sideways by the men who were clawing at him.

Two of the bandits threw themselves into the falling water and disappeared into the lake as another of the men closest to Iron Eyes raised his pistol and fired. The bullet passed through the long wet hair of the stunned bounty hunter. Gunsmoke burned at the flesh of his face as he pressed a boot on top of the bandit and pushed him back down.

Without a moment's hesitation, Iron Eyes blasted at the bandit, who fell backwards on top of another of the startled men. Trying to wipe the smouldering black powder from his face, Iron Eyes staggered backwards and tried to see where the man he had spotted next to the half-naked Rosie Smith had gone.

His question was answered: Malverez fired both his pistols at Iron Eyes.

The bounty hunter felt the heat of the bullets as they passed through his long trail-coat. Malverez was still next to the Smith girl and Iron Eyes knew he did not dare to return fire. He jumped down behind one of the large boxes filled with coins from the bandits' previous ransoms and swiftly reloaded his Navy Colt.

Another volley of bullets ripped the top of the boxes apart.

Iron Eyes was covered from head to foot in burning splinters of smouldering wood. Just as he was about to return fire he heard the screams of Rosie Smith and stopped.

'Help! Help!' came her pitiful calls.

Her voice echoed around the interior of the cave as Iron Eyes dropped down beside the boxes and tried to get another look, to see whether he could get a clean shot at Malverez.

It was impossible without risking hitting her.

Suddenly the bandit who had had his dead comrade fall upon him managed to crawl free. He rolled across the floor of the cave to a huge boulder. He scrambled behind it and blasted two shots off at Iron Eyes. Neither came close.

Bullets were flying at Iron Eyes from two different directions now. He was being kept pinned down in a crossfire.

The sound of gunshots came bouncing off the walls of the cave from outside. The bounty hunter glanced at the waterfall and knew that Sheriff Hardin and Black Ben were now busy with the two bandits who had escaped through the water.

It was a raging battle that he wished he was part of but he had to take care of two bandits here first.

Another shot tore the side of one of the treasure boxes apart and long wooden shavings stuck into Iron Eyes' face. He tore them out and saw the blood on his fingers.

Without a single thought for the bruised female, Malverez got to his feet and dragged the helpless Rosie backwards. He was using her as a shield. He continued walking backwards and firing until he reached the mouth of a tunnel carved by nature itself into the solid rock of the huge cave.

'Come on, gringo! Are you afraid?' Malverez shouted defiantly before pushing her aside. The bandit leader did not wait for a reply and disappeared into the passageway behind him. The cave was honeycombed with a maze of tunnels leading to dozens of places.

Only the bandits knew where they all led.

'Wait for me, *amigo*,' the other bandit called out to the vanishing heels of Malverez. There was no response. Malverez had gone.

Iron Eyes crawled back around the boxes until he could see what was going on inside the cave. He spotted the sobbing Rosie Smith lying next to the tunnel and then felt the heat of another bullet as the last remaining bandit blasted at him.

Dust covered the bounty hunter as he cocked his pistol again and fired. He heard the lead ball bounce off the large rock.

Iron Eyes dragged his aching left leg up underneath him and then steadied himself. He knew that the bandit was well hidden behind the boulder at the back of the cave and that it was impossible to get a clean shot at the man.

'Malverez?' the bandit's pathetic voice called out. He ought to have known better. Men like Malverez did not risk their lives for anyone. They took care of themselves. Only them-selves.

Iron Eyes pulled his other Navy Colt from his deep jacket-pocket and cocked its hammer before laying it on the ground next to his knee. Then he opened the chamber of the gun in his hand and emptied all its shells on to the floor of the cave. The bounty hunter was not a man who used trickery often but sometimes it was the swiftest way to resolve a problem.

And the bandit hidden twenty yards away between himself and the sobbing Rosie was a big problem.

Iron Eyes lifted the primed pistol up off the ground. He held it in his left hand as he leaned around the boxes, with the empty gun in his right hand.

He cocked its hammer and squeezed its trigger. The sound of the empty gun reached the ears of the bandit, who rose and fanned the hammer of his own gun at the treasure boxes.

Defying the bullets that were flying all around him, Iron Eyes raised his fully loaded Navy Colt and pulled back on its hammer until it locked.

Then he squeezed the trigger.

The bullet hit the bandit squarely in the centre of his chest, sending him spinning on his heels and crashing into the cave wall behind him. As the bandit's body slid down the wall, a red line of blood was left as a reminder of Iron Eyes' deadly accuracy.

Iron Eyes was about to move in the direction of the sobbing female when he realized that the battle outside the cave was still raging.

He loaded his Navy Colts hurriedly.

164

'Stay there, Miss Rosie,' Iron Eyes shouted across to the girl who was now lying on the ground near the tunnel. 'I'll be right back.'

Iron Eyes limped to the cave entrance and made his way out towards the sound of the gunfire. No sooner had the tall bounty hunter stepped away from the falling water than a bullet bounced off the cave wall.

Fine stone-dust covered Iron Eyes as he blasted both his guns in retaliation.

'Stay where you are, Iron Eyes,' Black Ben Tucker shouted from behind the cover of a tree.

'Where's Hardin?' Iron Eyes shouted back as he caught sight of the drenched bandits fifty yards ahead of him. They were pinned down.

'I'm OK,' the sheriff shouted from behind a pile of rocks near the water's edge.

Iron Eyes ducked as another bullet came too close to him for comfort. He pulled back the hammer of his left-hand pistol and fired once. The closest of the bandits' head burst with the impact of the lethal shot.

Iron Eyes felt his injured leg hurting and he stopped his advance. If the bandit wanted a showdown, he would have to bring it to him.

The other bandit turned his attention on Iron Eyes and fanned the hammer of his pistol repeatedly until it was empty.

The bandit dropped his gun and raised both his arms in the air and waved them around.

'He's finished!' Hardin exclaimed, coming out from behind his place of cover. He approached the bandit.

'He's finished OK,' Black Ben Tucker agreed, moving away from the tree he had been hiding behind.

Suddenly the bandit dropped both his arms and pulled another gun from inside his shirt. He fired straight at Tucker, sending the train-robber reeling on his heels. Hardin stopped in his tracks and squeezed the trigger of his Colt. It was empty.

The bandit fired again at the sheriff

and brought the older man down, clutching his forearm.

Instantly Iron Eyes' thumbs pulled back the hammers of both his Navy Colts a fraction of a second before his index fingers pulled the triggers.

Two bullets tore through the morning air and caught the Mexican high in his chest. The bandit was lifted off his feet and landed in the lake. A red cloud of blood encircled the floating body.

'You get the girl, Iron Eyes. I'm OK.' Tucker waved his arm at the grim-faced man.

Iron Eyes looked in the direction of Hardin. He was getting up from the ground.

'Get Rosie, son,' the lawman shouted.

Iron Eyes turned and entered the cave again. He somehow managed to make his way across the huge expanse and reach her far faster than a man in his condition should have. He knelt down and stared at the shaking female.

Her near-naked body made him turn his head. It had been a long time since he had seen a female looking so vulnerable and it confused him.

'Don't you worry none, Miss Rosie. Things will be OK.'

She recognized the voice of the man she had met only once in the streets of Cripple Creek.

'Is that you, Iron Eyes?'

'Yep.'

'I knew that if anyone could rescue me from these animals, it would be you.' Rosie grabbed the man and pulled him close. She could feel his heart pounding beneath his shirt. 'There was something in your voice. I knew that you were a good man.'

Iron Eyes seemed to find her attention flattering. He rose to his feet and moved over to the soiled velvet drape lying on the ground. Rosie would not loosen her grip on him for even a second as he bent down, lifted it and shook the dirt from it.

He wrapped it around her and then managed to force her away from him.

She appeared to have no idea of the

temptation her beautiful body could arouse in men. Without any thought of her upper body being naked she stepped closer to Iron Eyes again and allowed the drape to fall apart.

'I think that you're very special, Iron Eyes. You saved my life. I . . . I think that I . . . '

The tall bounty hunter touched her lips and stopped her talking. He knew what she was about to say and yet he did not want to hear it. Iron Eyes had travelled alone for far too long to even think about anyone as lovely as Jed Smith's daughter.

Iron Eyes pulled the velvet material together so that his eyes could no longer look at her body. No longer see her soft pale skin and imagine things that could never be.

'Are you OK, Miss Rosie?'

She nodded.

'He did things to me but I think you arrived just in the nick of time. Is he dead?'

'Not yet, Miss Rosie. But it's only a matter of time.'

'Time?' She tilted her head and stared at him with the beautiful blue eyes that he knew could not see him.

'I'll catch him and then he'll be with his friends in Hell.'

Just then the wounded Sheriff Tom Hardin staggered into the cave, clutching his lower left arm.

'She's safe!' the sheriff cried out joyfully.

'She is.' Iron Eyes led her to the side of the lawman and stared down at the blood-soaked shirt-sleeve. 'Are you OK?'

'Just winged, that's all,' Hardin replied.

The bounty hunter reached down into his pockets and found enough bullets to reload his Navy Colts. He looked at the tunnel that Malverez had disappeared into and wondered where it led.

'One of the varmints ran into there.' He pointed. 'Where do you figure it leads, Sheriff?'

'Maybe nowhere. He could be hiding

in there waiting for us to leave,' Hardin suggested, placing a comforting arm around Rosie's shoulder.

'Or there could be a tunnel leading back up to the top of the falls, Sheriff,' Iron Eyes said urgently.

'That's where them *hombres* left their horses,' Tom Hardin agreed. 'It would make sense for him to try and get back to their mounts.'

Iron Eyes tucked both his guns into his belt and started out of the cave.

'Look after her, Sheriff.'

'Where ya headed?' Hardin asked.

'After the bandit,' he replied. 'Stay here until I get back.'

Iron Eyes started out of the cave when the sound of Rosie Smith's voice filled his ears.

'I love you, Iron Eyes.'

The bounty hunter turned his head and looked back at her but did not reply. He had a bandit named Malverez to catch.

22

Black Ben Tucker nursed the deep gash in his side and helped the tall limping bounty hunter to the top of the narrow twisting trail. Iron Eyes held on to one of his trusty pistols and paused for breath as the wounded train-robber rested his back against a sturdy boulder. They had made their way up from the foot of the falls in good time, but it felt to the two injured men as if they had climbed a mountain.

Tucker panted heavily. 'This is loco.'

'You think everything's loco.' Iron Eyes ran his fingers through his hair and tried to collect his thoughts. Even now the poison from the Apache arrow still haunted him.

'You sure that there's a tunnel leading up here, Iron Eyes?' Tucker asked. Iron Eyes was squinting directly in the direction of the sun.

'Nope,' Iron Eyes replied honestly. He grabbed hold of the shorter man's arm and pulled Tucker along after him. They were headed back towards the wagon and horses.

'Then why are we in such a hurry?'

Iron Eyes shrugged.

''Coz if I am right and the bandit called Malverez has made his way up here, he'll either run our horses off or just shoot them so that we can't follow.'

'You make it sound logical but I'm bushed and hurting.'

'Hush up.' Iron Eyes dragged his companion after him along the edge of the steep cliff towards where they had left their horses.

Black Ben trailed the long-legged man through the thick undergrowth and noticed that Iron Eyes was hardly limping any longer.

'What the hell are you made of, Iron Eyes?' Black Ben Tucker asked as they reached the clearing where the six bandit horses had been tethered.

Iron Eyes did not reply. He just

forced the train-robber down on to his knees and cocked the hammer of his pistol. He knew that something was wrong.

'What's the matter, Iron Eyes?' Tucker asked.

Iron Eyes remained standing. He placed his left hand on top of Black Ben's Stetson and forced it down until he stopped talking.

'Hush up,' Iron Eyes ordered as he stood trying to work out where the bandit was.

Black Ben Tucker pushed his hat up off his head until he too could see the horses that were standing in a line fifty feet away from them.

'Wait,' Tucker said quietly as he counted the horses. 'I thought that there were six horses there. Now there are only five.'

'At least you can count. Stay there and cover me.' Iron Eyes made his way forward with his gun held firmly in his hand.

The tall man edged his way deeper

into the brush. He could smell the bandit was close. Just how close was something he would have to find out the hard way.

Then he heard it.

The sound of a gun hammer being primed into position.

Iron Eyes stopped walking and gazed into the thick green bushes which surrounded him completely. Malverez was near by and waiting for even a half-chance at shooting the tall lean figure who had invaded his world and destroyed his well-laid plans. He wanted nothing more than to kill him.

Neither man would be satisfied with anything less than the total destruction of the other.

Iron Eyes pulled his other Navy Colt from his belt and cocked its hammer. His screwed-up eyes searched the area for even a hint of where Malverez was. He had hurt the young female down in the cave and that was something that could never be forgiven.

Now he had two guns ready and able

to stop this evil creature from continuing his reign of terror.

He stepped forward slowly with his bony hands gripping his gun handles. He knew that Malverez was close enough to spit at and was holding his horse in check. But the nervous animal was breathing heavily, giving the hunter a direction in which to aim his pointed mule-ear boots.

Then he felt the venom of the lethal lead as it blasted at him. Branches were blown off the trees all around him but he did not pause even for a second.

Malverez had to be a lot more accurate than that if he wanted to stop Iron Eyes. For he now had the scent of his prey in his nostrils and nothing could stop him from continuing to hunt him down.

Nothing except death itself. But for the man who was like a living ghost, it was doubtful whether even death could stop him.

'You better run away, gringo,' Malverez's voice called out from deep in the dense brush. 'I will surely kill you if you do not.'

Iron Eyes heard the footsteps coming from behind him. To his sensitive ears, it sounded like an approaching cart-horse. He knew that it was Black Ben Tucker.

'You OK, Iron Eyes?'

'I told you to stay where you were,' Iron Eyes responded angrily.

'You might need my help,' Tucker said.

Iron Eyes shook his head.

'I read your Wanted poster, Black Ben. It said that you were a real good train-robber but there was nothing about you being a good shot.'

'There wasn't? Hell!' Black Ben looked almost hurt.

'Are you?' Iron Eyes gritted his teeth and studied the brush to their right. Even though it was only a hundred feet away, it was dried and withered. The spray of the waterfall did not seem to touch that place.

A place where the kindling was brittle

and cracked beneath the feet of anyone who walked over it. The way that Malverez was doing right now.

Quickly Iron Eyes took three steps forward with Black Ben at his side. He fired both guns at once and then pulled back the hammers of his Navy Colts again and waited for the gunsmoke to drift away from the clearing.

'Who you shooting at?' Black Ben asked.

Before Iron Eyes could answer the question he felt the heat of two more bullets cutting past him and then saw the train-robber being knocked off his feet. The sound of the gunfire echoed all around the tall bounty hunter.

Iron Eyes dropped down next to the man who had saved his life a mere dozen or so hours earlier. A man whom he had trailed with the intention of killing for the bounty on his head. A man whom he had grown to like.

The bounty hunter rammed one of his guns into his pocket and stared down at the large hole in the middle of the wide-eyed train robber.

Black Ben was finished and both men knew it.

'You're hurt bad, Black Ben.'

'I figured that out myself, Iron Eyes.'

'You didn't answer my question, Black Ben.'

'What question was that?' Tucker tried to lift his head up from the grass but failed. He stared into the face of the man whom he had grown to respect.

'Are you a good shot?' Iron Eyes pulled the blood-soaked shirt-front over the gaping hole in the man's midriff.

'Nope.' Tucker forced a smile. 'Never could get the hang of hitting things with a gun.'

Iron Eyes patted the shoulder of the train-robber.

'Stay here. I'm gonna kill that bastard Malverez.'

Black Ben Tucker coughed and tasted the blood in his mouth. He watched Iron Eyes run back and untie the reins of one of the bandit horses. The bounty hunter sank his spurs into the unsuspecting mount and thundered straight at the dried-up thicket.

Both his guns were blasting.

'I ain't going nowhere,' Tucker mumbled to himself.

23

As the wide-eyed horse crashed through the wall of dry branches, Iron Eyes hauled his reins up to his chest and stared angrily out at the white sand to the south. He could see the dust rising off the hoofs of the bandit leader's mount as it sped deeper into the barren Mexican wasteland.

Without a second thought, the bounty hunter thrashed both sides of the horse with the ends of the long reins and forced the animal on.

Iron Eyes stood in the stirrups and thundered across the dried brush and out on to the sand at a pace that no other rider could have managed to urge from the bandit horse. His razor-sharp spurs jabbed deep into the flesh of the mount until it gathered pace and was racing at full speed.

With every stride that the horse

beneath him made, Iron Eyes could see Malverez getting closer.

He was gaining on the bandit with every beat of his heart and knew that it was only a matter of time before he was within range. Malverez was going to have to pay dearly for the violation of Rosie Smith and the gunning down of Black Ben Tucker, he thought.

But unlike that of any of the other men he had hunted over the years, this was not going to be a swift neat killing that he would unleash.

Iron Eyes wanted to make this man suffer.

He would extract his own brand of justice slowly.

The horse galloped faster and faster after the fleeing Mexican bandit as if trying to get away from the vicious spurs of the determined bounty hunter.

Yet there was no escaping them.

Iron Eyes drove them deep into the animal, knowing that this was the only way he would ever catch up with Malverez.

As both riders climbed the soft sandy rise that led to the desert, Iron Eyes aimed and fired one of his Navy Colts.

Malverez's horse collapsed suddenly, sending its rider flying over its head into the sand.

Iron Eyes continued to force his mount up the steep soft incline until he reached the grounded bandit. The bounty hunter aimed the nose of the skittish mount straight at Malverez as he tried desperately to rise to his feet. Iron Eyes pulled his left boot from its stirrup and leapt from his saddle on top of the stunned man.

Even Malverez had never seen such an unholy-looking adversary before. With his long black hair flowing behind the collar of his trail-coat and his bloodstained face with eyes the colour of bullets, the bandit suddenly realized that this was one gringo he should never have encountered.

Iron Eyes felt the hot lead of the bandit's pistol as it fired at him. The bullets had torn through the skin beneath his arm but that did not stop him. He crashed down on to the man heavily and smashed a fist into the unshaven jaw.

Malverez fell back into the soft white sand and tried to fire again. Iron Eyes squeezed the trigger of his right-hand Navy Colt and watched as half the bandit's hand was blown off.

The desert was filled with the screams of the bandit as he vainly tried to reach his other gun with his left hand.

Once again, Iron Eyes blasted at the other hand with his trusty Colt. Fingers flew off in all directions as Malverez yelled out in agony.

Iron Eyes heard none of the pitiful pleas for mercy. There was no mercy in the soul of the bounty hunter as he felt his own blood trickling down from beneath his arm.

He was about to fire again when an arrow landed at his feet and made Iron Eyes look up towards the top of a nearby sandy dune a hundred yards away.

'Ochawas!' Iron Eyes gasped in horror as he looked across at the five remaining Apache braves whom he had encountered the previous day.

He had found out the hard way about their poisonous arrowheads and did not want to repeat what he had gone through when hit by one.

The Apaches were yelling out as they drove their painted ponies down the dune towards him.

With a last full-blooded kick of his boot into the face of the bandit, Iron Eyes turned and grabbed the reins and saddle horn of the horse and threw himself on to its back. Arrows flew over his head as the bounty hunter galloped back in the direction of the waterfall.

When he had covered a quarter of a mile, Iron Eyes turned his head and stared over his shoulder through the rising dust behind his horse. The Ochawas had found what was left of Malverez and were doing to him what Iron Eyes felt certain they would have done to him, if he had not driven his horse out of there at top speed.

Most men would have felt pity at the sight that he witnessed as he galloped away from the Apaches.

But Iron Eyes felt only anger.

He had been robbed of the chance to finish Malverez off and it riled him. He had been cheated of torturing the bandit the way that ruthless kidnapper had done to so many of his victims.

Iron Eyes had wanted to extract every ounce of the man's blood from his worthless veins personally.

Yet as he rode the exhausted horse back into the brush at the top of the waterfall and saw Black Ben lying helplessly on the blood-soaked sand, Iron Eyes knew that the Ochawas were probably far better at inflicting death than he was himself.

He was used to killing swiftly and they had made an art of doing the exact opposite.

Dismounting, Iron Eyes rushed to the side of Tucker and knelt down.

'I got the varmint, Black Ben.'

Iron Eyes suddenly realized that Black Ben Tucker could not hear him. He was quite dead and yet the face still had a hint of the roguish smile that had endeared him to Iron Eyes. The thin bony fingers of the bounty hunter closed the lifeless eyes and he sighed heavily.

Why had Black Ben saved the life of a total stranger? Iron Eyes pondered.

Black Ben Tucker knew the answer, but he had taken it to his maker. It would remain a secret until their trails crossed again in wherever it is that train-robbers and bounty hunters go once death finally claims them.

He began to dig into the soft sand with his bare hands. Iron Eyes was going to bury the man whom he knew was worth $2,000 dead or alive.

This was one bounty he was not willing to collect.

Finale

Iron Eyes had felt certain that darkness was the best time to return the beautiful Rosie Smith to her father. The hours after sundown offered a little more privacy and dignity to one who had suffered so much at the hands of the men he had destroyed. There were no prying eyes peering through lace curtains or around corners to see her arriving back with her torn dress that was barely capable of concealing her blushes.

Iron Eyes had sent Sheriff Tom Hardin back to Cripple Creek a couple of hours earlier to tell Jed Smith that all was well.

With his dapple-grey tied to the tail-gate of the wagon, Iron Eyes had sat next to the beautiful female for hours as he steered the four-horse team back across the border towards her home town.

For hours she had sat next to him covered in the remains of her once-pristine dress and the heavy velvet drape. Mile after mile she had leaned into the shoulder of the man whom she felt so drawn to.

The man who, she knew, had saved her from a fate worse than death and possibly even death itself.

Rosie Smith had not stopped talking for even a fleeting moment of their long journey as she clung to his arm. Perhaps, he thought, she was in shock. Maybe she always talked to people this way, or was it because she actually believed that she did love the tall stranger?

Iron Eyes slapped the reins down on to the backs of the team of horses and steered them slowly and quietly into the boundaries of Cripple Creek.

He knew which of the small town's streets were the least likely to be busy and guided the team down them. As they turned the last corner and headed into the street where her large home was situated, Iron Eyes felt her gripping his hands and pulling back on the reins.

'Stop, Iron Eyes,' she said, with panic in her soft young voice. 'We have to talk.'

Iron Eyes rested his right boot on the brake-pole and held the horses in check.

'You ain't stopped talking since we headed out for here, Miss Rosie,' he told her.

'We are only a short way from my home,' Rosie said.

'How do you know that?' Iron Eyes felt her hand touching his face in the darkness and swallowed hard as her fingers traced his scarred features.

'I can smell the honeysuckle,' Rosie continued touching his face with her soft gentle fingers. He liked it. 'You have been in many, many fights. I can feel all the scars that you have suffered over the years.'

Iron Eyes tried to pull her hands away from his face but she just hugged him around the neck instead and whispered into his ear.

'I meant it, you know. I do love you. I have done since the moment we first met outside my home.'

Iron Eyes pulled her arms off him and looked hard into her face. He still found it hard to grasp that such beautiful eyes could not see.

'You're just grateful that I saved you, Miss Rosie.'

'No, Iron Eyes. I really do love you.'

'If'n you could see what I look like, you'd not say that.'

She touched his face again.

'Maybe I can see some things that folks with vision can't see, Iron Eyes.'

He shook his head, released the brake-pole and encouraged the horses to continue down the dark, quiet street.

As the wagon pulled up outside the white picket-fence, Iron Eyes stopped it again and wrapped the long reins around the brake-pole. He climbed down and then used his long arms to reach up to her and pluck her from the passenger seat.

He held her in his arms and stared into her face for what felt like an eternity. Then he turned and walked through the open gateway and towards the front door of the large house. A mere two steps from the door, she buried her lips on his.

She kissed him with every ounce of the love she had proclaimed for the tall bounty hunter. He allowed her to do so and savoured every moment until the door began to open. He had never been kissed by anyone before and doubted that it would ever happen again.

Only as the light of the lamps from inside the house splashed out on to the garden, did Iron Eyes pull his mouth away from hers.

Jed Smith came rushing out with Tom Hardin at his side. The banker took her from the arms of the bounty hunter and began to weep with utter relief.

'How can I ever thank you, Iron Eyes?' Smith asked as he took his daughter inside the house. 'Name it and it's yours.'

Iron Eyes nodded silently at the banker and then patted the sheriff on his shoulder before turning around and walking back towards the street.

'Iron Eyes! Where are you going? Don't go!' Rosie's voice called out as he reached the back of the wagon. He unhitched his reins and led his dapple-grey silently past the house.

'What's wrong, Rosie?' Jed Smith asked his daughter as tears rolled from her eyes.

'Don't let him go, Father! Please! I want him to stay!'

Iron Eyes stepped into his stirrup and mounted the horse. He looked at the beautiful young female for the last time and then tapped his spurs into the sides of his horse.

Sheriff Hardin lowered his head as Iron Eyes disappeared into the darkness of night. He knew how hard it must have been for the bounty hunter to do that simple thing. He wondered if he could have had the strength to do the same.

A TOWN CALLED TROUBLESOME

John Dyson

Matt Matthews had carved his ranch out of the wild Wyoming frontier. But he had his troubles. The big blow of '86 was catastrophic, with dead beeves littering the plains, and the oncoming winter presaged worse. On top of this, a gang of desperadoes had moved into the Snake River valley, killing, raping and rustling. All Matt can do is to take on the killers single-handed. But will he escape the hail of lead?

RODEO RENEGADE

Ty Kirwan

When English couple Rufus and Nancy Medford inherit a ranch in New Mexico, they find the majority of their neighbours are hostile to strangers. Befriended by only one rancher, and plagued by rustlers, the thought of returning to England is tempting, but needing to prove himself, Rufus is coached as a fighter by a circus sharp shooter, the mysterious Ghost of the Cimarron. But will this be enough to overcome the frightening odds against him?

CABEL

Paul K. McAfee

Josh Cabel returned home from the Civil War to find his family all murdered by rioting members of Quantrill's band. The hunt for the killers led Josh to Colorado City where, after months of searching, he finally settled down to work on a ranch nearby. He saved the life of an Indian, who led him to a cache of weapons waiting for Sitting Bull's attack on the Whites. His involvement threw Cabel into grave danger. When the final confrontation came, who had the fastest — and deadlier — draw?

RIVERBOAT

Alan C. Porter

When Rufus Blake died he was found to be carrying a gold bar from a Confederate gold shipment that had disappeared twenty years before. This inspires Wes Hardiman and Ben Travis to swap horse and trail for a riverboat, the *River Queen*, on the Mississippi, in an effort to find the missing gold. Cord Duval is set on destroying the *River Queen* and he has the power and the gunmen to do it. Guns blaze as Hardiman and Travis attempt to unravel the mystery and stay alive.

McKINNEY'S LAW

Mike Stotter

McKinney didn't count on coming across a dead body in the middle of Texas. He was about to become involved in an ever-deepening mystery. The renegade Comanche warrior, Black Eagle, was on the loose, creating havoc; he didn't appear in McKinney's plans at all, not until the Comanche forced himself into his life. The US Army gave McKinney some relief to his problems, but it also added to them, and with two old friends McKinney set about bringing justice through his own law.

BLACK RIVER

Adam Wright

John Dyer has come to the insignificant little town of Black River to destroy the last living reminder of his dark past. He has come to kill. Jack Hart is determined to stop him. Only he knows the terrible truth that has driven Dyer here, and he knows that only he can beat Dyer in a gunfight. Ex-lawman Brad Harris is after Dyer too — to avenge his family. The stage is set for madness, death and vengeance.

CLARE AND EFFIE

Don Gress⌁

CLARE AND EFFIE

Merryn Williams

With Illustrations by Bernice Carlill

HONNO CHILDREN'S FICTION

Published by Honno
'Ailsa Craig', Heol y Cawl,
Dinas Powys CF6 4AH
Wales

British Library Cataloguing in Publication Data

A catalogue record for this book is available
from the British Library

ISBN 1 870206 19 3

*Published with the financial support of the
Arts Council of Wales*

Cover design by Emma Veitch
Typeset and printed in Wales by Dinefwr Press, Llandybïe

THE BEGINNING

Clare was painting.

A fat, yellow pear, bursting with juice, sat on her dressing-table, and she was struggling to get the colour just right. You couldn't use pure yellow, you had to darken it with little brown flecks so you got the look of a real pear. So people would think they could lift it off the paper and sink their teeth in it.

Her parents were quarrelling in their bedroom across the landing. Again.

She leant back, decided the picture was good, and wrote her name CLARE DRUMMOND in the bottom left corner. Later she'd colour the grey paper green so the pear would stand out clearly. She might not be brilliant, like her brother Jamie, but he couldn't paint and she could. Perhaps, and this was a dream she'd never told anybody, one day she'd be famous and have her pictures in museums like Great-Uncle Cornelius. Cornelius who had been the genius of her family, or at least the greatest genius before Jamie.

The trouble was, you couldn't paint properly, or do anything else, when your parents kept screaming at each other.

'Anne, I don't want to quarrel.' Her father's voice, with the Welsh accent she and Jamie made fun of. He sounded totally exhausted.

'You don't want to quarrel,' mother said coldly, 'you only want to sponge off me.'

Shut up, Clare prayed, please shut up.

'That's not fair!'

'So what is? I was happy to go out to work while you were unemployed –'

'Go on,' Dad said, 'rub my nose in it.'

'But I did resent it when I came home and you'd done absolutely nothing. It's the same nowadays when I come back from Swansea. The house filthy, the children running wild, you lying around watching TV in your dressing-gown –'

'Oh, hell!' Dad shouted, and Clare guessed he was changing the subject because he knew he was in the wrong. 'Why do you keep going to Wales anyway? You know that woman isn't ever going to get better.'

'Don't call my mother *that woman*.'

'Well, she is a woman, isn't she? Her mind's gone, she'll never be the same person again. I think you've been neglecting your own family – '

'*I* neglect the family?' Mother usually grew colder and quieter as Dad got more worked up, but this time she seemed outraged. 'I do the cooking and cleaning, Tom. I visit the children's schools and help Clare with her homework because you're always somewhere else. I also have a demanding job, which I can't afford to give up. And then you walk in late at night, fresh from drinks with the boys, and tell me all about your hard day – '

'Oh shut up, you – !'

Clare stuffed her fingers in her ears but she couldn't help hearing. It was awful; she wished they were a disc she could turn off. And only a year ago, everything had been fine. If only Dad hadn't lost his job and been unemployed for months, and had to see the doctor for depression. He'd got another job now, but it meant commuting to London and anyway he wasn't happy with it, she knew. Or if Grandma far away in Swansea hadn't begun behaving oddly, so that Mother had to go there at weekends, leaving her and Jamie with Dad. That was fun, actually. Dad let them sit up half the night watching horror films, and instead of cooking they'd go out and buy pizzas and curries and masses of ice-cream. But Mother always looked horrified when she came in, pale and dazed from the long journey, at the sight of the mess and dirty dishes.

That was Mother's voice again – 'Bone-idle and selfish. You won't wash up or clean a floor because it's too difficult, but I'm expected to cope with everything that comes along. It's getting too much, Tom. If it were just myself and the children I think I could manage, but I also have to wait hand and foot on you. I can't – '

'Oh, God, I've had as much as I can take!' Dad shouted, and then Clare heard him erupt out of the room and down the stairs, Mother making no effort to go after him.

The front door slammed. She tore the lovely pear in half and threw it in the bin.

CHAPTER 1

One year later, Clare was finishing a portrait of her best friend, Minnie, along with the rest of her class. Minnie sat in front with a red shawl draped round her shoulders, and giggled each time someone caught her eye. But Clare was concentrating deeply. This was going to be her best picture, the best ever.

Miss Hobbs came up.

'That's beautiful, Clare!' she said, and Clare could tell from her voice that she meant it. 'Come here, everyone, have a look!'

The class all looked and agreed that it was good, and Minnie got down from the platform and said she liked it, too.

'It runs in my family,' Clare said, trying to sound modest. 'My great-great-uncle was a famous painter.'

'What was his name?'

'Cornelius Price.'

'Never heard of him.'

'Well, I have,' Miss Hobbs said. 'He was very famous when I was a young girl.' (She was about sixty.) 'Are you sure he was your uncle, Clare?'

'Positive. We've got a book about him at home.'

'Well, you must bring it to school tomorrow,' Miss Hobbs said as the bell rang.

Walking home in the sticky July heat, Clare decided that her day had been perhaps a little better than usual. Minnie, whose real name was Catherine Minnister, had talked about having a swimming party, and it was a change for Miss Hobbs to say anything nice. Only yesterday she'd heard her whispering to another teacher, 'Clare's work has gone to pieces this year. It's a shame – '

And he'd replied, 'You'd never think she was Jamie's sister.'

Jamie. Always Jamie who had gone triumphantly through the school three years ahead of her, and won all the prizes, and whom everyone liked so much because he was so nice and polite, and mature.

The suburb was called Peacock Hill. It was a lovely name but not a lovely place, just an estate on the edge of Milton Keynes with a supermarket and several hundred houses, all built in ugly dark red brick. They'd gone up only ten years ago but they were already looking scruffy. She turned into her own street and saw the billboards had been changed; they'd taken down the one with the girl draped over the white car and put up one for Marlboro cigarettes.

She got her key out and let herself in. Mother would be back in an hour from the school where she taught maths. Dad was living in a room over the bookshop at Chalk Farm. Her brother was already home and reading his report.

'Hello, Earwig. You can see this if you like,' he said graciously.

Jamie was looking white and saucer-eyed, having

6

been working flat out for the last six months for GCSE. His results were not known yet but of course would all be As, and he'd also found time to appear on a children's TV show and captain the school team at volley-ball. Clare glanced at his report, while their new black kitten, Persephone, came up and rubbed her legs.

'*James has done outstanding work.*'

'*James is a valued member of the school.*'

'*Well done, James!*'

And so on.

'Got yours yet?' Jamie asked.

'No,' Clare said, 'tomorrow.'

She wasn't looking forward to that. She chewed her lip and stared at the Cornelius Price picture over the mantel which Mother said was worth more than anything else in the house. It showed a brilliant blue pool and a young woman lying beside it wearing almost nothing.

'Anyway, I'm going to be top in art.' That 'Anyway' meant bottom in everything else. 'Miss Hobbs was looking at my picture of Minnie, and she likes it. I think I might be an artist when I grow up.'

'There aren't any women artists,' said Jamie.

'Why not?'

'They haven't got the talent.'

'That's not true!'

'Well, can you name a single painter who was a woman?'

Clare thought. She couldn't.

'I can name at least ten artists,' Jamie went on

with his annoying smile, 'and they're all men. There's Rembrandt, and Van Gogh, Cornelius of course, Monet, Manet, Leonardo da Vinci, Constable, Turner, Picasso, Andy Warhol – '

'Oh, shut up!' Clare bounced off the sofa and put on the TV, then closed the curtains to exclude the bright sunshine. 'I want to watch!'

Jamie went on grinning but said no more. Clare folded her feet back under her and sat on the floor, glaring. She'd been feeling quite good when she came home, and now Jamie had made her feel awful again. Everything had been awful for the last year.

She thought, I've been alive for twelve years and this one has been worse than all the rest put together. First, her parents splitting up. Minnie said you got used to it after a while but she hadn't, she never would. Then their old cat, Rasputin, had died. They'd found him stiff and cold in a neighbour's garden one February morning, and Jamie had been so upset that he'd lain down on the floor and howled. She had howled, too, and Mother had had to get them a new kitten. Then Grandma had died too, a month ago. They hadn't been so upset about her because she was very old and odd and lived a long way away but still, it was one more bad thing. They were going to stay in her house this summer to clear it before it was sold. It might have been fun to have a holiday by the sea; it was just unfortunate that Jamie was coming too.

When their mother got home they were peacefully

watching 'Neighbours'. She put down her briefcase and the two bags of shopping and dropped into the nearest chair.

'Nice to see you not fighting. Jamie, please put the kettle on.'

Jamie ignored her.

'I will,' Clare said, leaping up.

Their mother was a small woman, distinctly smaller than Jamie who had shot up in the last year. She looked rather like him, having the same regular features, hazel eyes and smooth dark hair. Clare was big for her age and very fair like Dad.

'Mother,' she said when she came out from the kitchen, 'Miss Hobbs said my painting of Minnie was brilliant.'

Jamie snorted. Mother said, 'That's nice.'

'And I told them about Cornelius.'

'Had they heard of him?'

'Miss Hobbs had. She was quite impressed.'

'Good.'

'I could take the picture to school, if it was a bit smaller. Why have we only got the one? He painted hundreds, didn't he?'

'We're not his real family, Clare. Cornelius was married three times and he had eight children, so most of his paintings belong to them.' She added, 'That woman is his second wife, Marguerite. I remember her as a dreadful old battleaxe in a black helmet. She's dead now, of course.'

Clare glanced up at the smiling girl beside the blue pool.

'So how are we related?'

Mother said, 'Cornelius was the eldest of three children. He had a sister, Euphemia, and a much younger brother, Archibald, who was my grandfather.'

'Cornelius, Euphemia and Archibald!' Jamie said scornfully. 'What gruesome names!'

Clare was about to ask a question when the kettle whistled and she dashed out to make tea. When she got back she dumped the tray and opened the curtains, then shrieked loudly.

'Mother! What have you done to your eye?'

Now that light was flooding into the room it was obvious that her mother was looking rather pale and one eye was swollen.

'It's nothing,' Mother said. 'Well, nothing I can't cope with.' Both children were staring at her now and this seemed to embarrass her. 'Slogger Brown hit me, that's all.'

They knew Slogger, a hulking boy who lounged around the pubs and under the bridges of the new town. He'd be twice the size of Mother, Clare thought.

'He and his friends were smoking in the playground and I asked them to stop. He started swearing, I told him not to use that language in school and that was when he hit me.' She didn't seem anxious to talk about it.

'I'll kill him!' Jamie shouted suddenly.

Clare was crying.

'Don't fuss,' Mother said. 'As you can see, I'm all

right. Clare, please stop that frightful noise and we'll have tea.'

'Just listen to her,' Jamie said disgustedly. He'd got over the first shock, but he still looked upset. 'She's twelve and she behaves as if she was *five*. What are they going to do to him, Mum?'

Mother shrugged. 'Nothing, basically. He's about to leave anyway. And the Head doesn't want everyone to know what goes on in his school. So there's nothing to be done, unless I want to go to the police. Which I don't.'

'Why not?'

'Oh,' Mother said, 'Slogger's bad enough now but if he went to Borstal that would really finish him. He's been told not to show his face near the school again, that's enough. Anyway, if I did that we might have to hang around here and miss going to Wales on Saturday.' She added in a curiously intense tone, 'I want to get away.'

Clare was so upset that Mother told her to go to bed early, with a good book. But she fell asleep almost as soon as her head hit the pillow. She only remembered when she woke up, in the middle of the night, that she'd intended to ask Mother about Cornelius's sister.

CHAPTER 2

The next day was the last day of term.

Clare took her Cornelius book to school, but she found that Miss Hobbs had already got one, called *A Dictionary of Modern Painters*. She showed her the entry for her great-great-uncle, which read:

PRICE, Cornelius, 1880–1963. The son of a Swansea solicitor, he was one of the leading British painters between the wars. Famous for his nudes and his Portrait of Winston Churchill. *His flamboyant private life made him a legend in his time. Lived in Sussex. Paintings in the Tate, National Museum of Wales, Museum of Modern Art etc.'*

'"Famous for his nudes"!' Minnie quoted, giggling. 'He must have been a nasty old man.'

'Not at all,' Miss Hobbs said. 'Painters are expected to draw nudes. That's why there were no women, because they weren't allowed – Yes, Mark?'

'What's flamboyant, Miss?'

Clare explained. 'He had three wives, and he used to sleep under the stars, and grew a long beard and wore colourful clothes. That sort of thing.'

They passed round her book, a big one with colour plates, which had been published soon after

Cornelius died. The blue pool, some women with no clothes on, *Portrait of D. H. Lawrence*, *Portrait of Winston Churchill*. The old man had known all the right people, it seemed.

Then they started clearing up in readiness for the summer holidays.

'Are you coming round tomorrow?' Minnie asked.

'Sorry, I can't. We're getting up very early to go to Swansea. We're going to live there all summer,' Clare said, 'and go to the beach, and clear out Gran's house.'

'Who's going? Your Dad?'

'No, just me, Mum and Jamie. I'd be looking forward to it only he's so nasty to me.' Clare hadn't meant to tell anyone how she felt about Jamie, but it spilled out. 'The only person he seems to like is Persephone.'

'Persephone isn't a person.'

'Well, you know what I mean. He was awful even before Dad left, but now he's loathsome.'

At the end of the day Miss Hobbs gave Clare her report. She read it on the way home:

'*Clare must try harder.*'

'*Clare has had a disappointing year.*'

'*Clare does not seem prepared to work at all.*'

And so on.

Mother had said she'd try to get home early, but she rang to say she had a meeting and that they could make their own meal if they wanted. 'And don't *fight*,' she ended up.

'You can make supper, Earwig,' Jamie said condescendingly.

'Don't call me *Earwig*!' Clare snapped back, but it was a nice idea. Mother hardly ever gave her the run of the kitchen.

She opened a tin of beans, cut herself, shrieked loudly until Jamie got a bandage. Then she heated them in a saucepan while she was making batter, scattering flour and eggshells everywhere. Then she found she'd burned the beans. Then she fried a giant pancake, but instead of coming out crisp and yellow it stuck to the pan and didn't taste very nice. They smothered it in raspberry jam and ate it anyway.

Afterwards Jamie said he was still hungry, and went out and bought two ice-creams from the van. They sat under the Cornelius picture, licking them.

'Mum's going to be fed up when she sees the kitchen,' Jamie remarked, stroking Persephone's ears.

'You could wash up,' Clare said hopefully.

'No chance. You made the mess, you deal with it.'

Clare thought maybe it would help if she ran some water into the burned pans, so she went into the kitchen and did it.

'I'll tell you one thing,' Jamie's voice followed her. 'It was never like this before Mum went back to work.'

Clare tried to think: it was too long ago.

'She ought to have stayed at home and looked after us.'

14

'That's sexist,' Clare said.

'Really, Earwig, you're always using words you don't know the meaning of.' Jamie's face looked greyish-white under the floppy dark hair. 'Everything was all right between her and Dad, until that happened.'

Clare didn't answer, just went back to her place in the window seat and tried to remember. Yes, for a long time it had been all right. Her parents had been happy when she was a small child; she was quite sure of that. Other people's parents got divorced, but she had never thought hers would. So when had it started to go wrong?

Well, she knew it had been agreed that Mother should go back to work, because Dad was unemployed and they needed the money. She'd said teaching was the perfect job because she could be at home at the same time as her and Jamie, but somehow that hadn't worked out. There were meetings after school and, when she finally got home, piles of marking. And Dad wasn't good around the house, he never had been. Looking back, she thought he hadn't liked it that Mum was earning when he wasn't. But maybe they could have managed, could have all pulled together, if Grandma hadn't started to go downhill at the same time. She was Mother's mother, the only real relation they'd got, since Dad's parents and brother had emigrated to New Zealand twenty years ago. She lived by herself in Swansea, her husband having died before Clare and Jamie were born. They used to visit her every summer until she began to get peculiar.

She wasn't ill in her body, Mother said, but because she was so old things were going wrong with her mind. She wouldn't leave the house where she'd spent her entire life or allow anyone to move in with her, and would scream through the letter-box at the social workers who banged on her door. But there was nothing anybody could do, because she was still able to look after herself, just. Mother was always on the phone, or rushing over at weekends to check on her, leaving the children with their father. That was when Dad had started saying that she was neglecting her family for the old lady.

Then she understood that her parents were having quarrels, mostly at night after she was in bed. She'd lie there listening to the distant sound of shouting. One morning she came down to find the mirror in pieces because Dad had broken it. It became quite horrible to sit through meals, with their arguments and their strained silences. Mother said there was nothing wrong, but she sometimes locked herself in her bedroom and cried quietly. And it had ended with that awful row when Dad stormed out. So when Grandma finally died, on a hot June day in the middle of Jamie's exams, it had been eleven months too late.

Clare stared out of the window, at the happy-looking people on the billboard sipping drinks and climbing into expensive cars. She'd heard someone say that when two people couldn't get on together their children were happier if they split up. Only it was a whole year since the split, and she wasn't happy. Not that she wanted to live in a house where there were always quarrels (she'd got that anyway, with Jamie). She wanted to go back to the time before there were quarrels, but there was obviously no chance of that. That time was dead, like the girl in Cornelius's painting; she was travelling further and further away from it and one day, perhaps, she'd stop feeling upset. But all she knew now was that this was the start of the holidays and she wasn't even looking forward to them; she could only think of how much fun it used to be, when they'd all piled into Dad's ancient car and driven to Wales together through the short summer night, to the white house overlooking Swansea Bay.

Mother got home at seven. She flinched when she saw the kitchen, but immediately started organizing them to tidy their bedrooms and pack. They were taking virtually everything they needed for the summer, except food and sheets, which they'd find at the other end. It wasn't until after dark that they could look at the pile of luggage and relax.

'I think we've done it all,' Mother said. 'Anyway, that's all I'm going to do! If Tom doesn't like the state of the house, he can clean it.'

Their father was going to move back for the summer while they were away. Persephone was coming with them. Of course it would be horrendous taking her on the train, but Jamie refused to leave her and anyway, knowing Dad, he'd probably forget her meals.

At seven the alarm shrilled and they got up, snatched a quick breakfast and drove to Central Milton Keynes station. They left the car there for Dad to pick up, then piled into the London train with minutes to spare.

It was going to be a long journey. Clare got out her giant pad and crayons while Jamie opened Persephone's box. She seemed surprised to find herself in a moving carriage but after a certain amount of rushing around she settled down. They thrust her back in again whenever the train stopped.

Through London, and along the Circle line to Paddington. Then onto the Swansea train and they were off, getting a glimpse of the Uffington White Horse outside Swindon and then plunging into the Severn Tunnel which separated England from Wales.

She'd almost forgotten what it was like, because she and Jamie hadn't been there for three years. It had been impossible for them to visit Grandma when she was behaving so strangely, and Mother hadn't taken them to the funeral but had rushed there and back in twenty-four hours. Newport, then Cardiff, finally they were pulling into Swansea station. They'd been on the same train for ages. It stopped and they tumbled out onto the platform, which was full of people talking in Welsh accents like Mother's. She and Jamie carried two heavy suitcases each and Clare carried Persephone. They struggled into the open air and passed a line of taxis.

'Can't we get this instead of the bus?'

'Oh well – just once.'

Soon the taxi was taking them out of the crowded city centre and along Oystermouth Road. They passed the new university buildings and caught their first glimpse of the lovely bay, blue in the afternoon sun. Three miles along the coast, they at last saw Grandma's house – an old-fashioned house, painted white.

The garden overlooked the sea. It was full of foxgloves and yellow roses, and the grass hadn't been cut for some time. There was a faint smell.

Clare rushed round exploring. It was a big house, much too big for one old lady, although Mother said it had been full of children, a long time ago. The rooms were huge and high with heavy marble mantels and fireplaces with old-fashioned picture tiles. Everything was in a mess, because Grandma obviously hadn't coped very well in her last years, but she could see it would be lovely once it was cleaned. When she'd stayed here before she'd always had a bedroom on the top floor, with a view of the bay. She rushed upstairs and dropped her coat and case on the bed.

Yes, this was the room she wanted. It was very cold and probably hadn't been slept in for years, but it had a marvellous view and, unlike the rest of the house, there was no smell.

Right, she thought, I'll ask Mother to keep Jamie out of this room. Coming out, she saw a picture on the wall of the dark landing, which she'd run straight past.

A girl in a red shawl against a dull gold background. She was holding a black cat – not unlike Persephone – on her knees, and she was staring out of the canvas with a wounded expression, as if yearning for something she wasn't going to get.

The colours were all muted, faint red, faint gold, faint black of the cat and the girl's hair. They seemed to be fading into the dark wall, almost as if they were about to disappear while she looked.

Had she seen it before? She must have if it had been hanging there on her last visit, but perhaps she hadn't been looking. And yet it did feel, somehow, like a picture she'd known all her life. One she really liked.

She walked slowly back into the kitchen where her mother was boiling a kettle.

'Mother, have you seen the picture of the girl with the cat? Did Cornelius do it?'

'Oh no,' her mother said. 'It isn't in Cornelius's style at all. That picture's by Effie.'

CHAPTER 3

'Who was Effie?' asked Clare.

She and Mother were sitting in the kitchen drinking tea without milk while Jamie occupied the drawing-room, watching TV. The house still smelled stale, although Mother had thrown open all the windows.

'Euphemia, Cornelius's sister. She was a painter too.'

'You never told me that.'

'Well, Clare, you never seemed very interested. None of Archie's branch of the family ever has been.' In response to Clare's questioning look she explained, 'Archie was my grandfather. He was much younger than the other two.'

'Tell me about Effie.'

Mother sighed. 'It's a long story, and I don't know much anyway.'

'Perhaps you'd better draw me a family tree,' Clare suggested, 'because it's confusing, with all these names.'

'All right,' Mother agreed. 'Only I won't put in all Cornelius's descendants, I don't remember half of them.'

She picked up an old envelope addressed to Grandma and drew a plan on the back in pencil.

'There, you see. There were these two children, Cornelius and Effie, living in this house with their

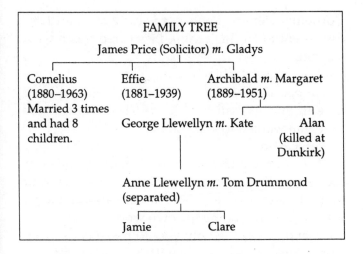

FAMILY TREE

James Price (Solicitor) *m.* Gladys

Cornelius (1880–1963) Married 3 times and had 8 children.

Effie (1881–1939)

Archibald *m.* Margaret (1889–1951)

George Llewellyn *m.* Kate

Alan (killed at Dunkirk)

Anne Llewellyn *m.* Tom Drummond (separated)

Jamie   Clare

parents about a hundred years ago. I think it was their mother who taught them drawing – '

'They lived in *this* house?'

'Yes. It's been in my family for four generations.'

'Go on.'

'Well, I don't think the parents were especially talented people, but their mother had painted water-colours before she was married and perhaps Cornelius and his sister took after her. But in 1889 she had another baby, Archie, and a week later she caught scarlet fever and died. Women did in those days.'

'How awful!'

'Yes. Their father got an aunt to keep house for him and she was more interested in the baby than the two older children. They were both rather wild, but they loved painting. When he was older

23

Cornelius went to London to study art, and later Effie went too. I don't think they cared much what she did.'

'What about Archie?'

'He became a solicitor, like his father, and lived here in Swansea all his life. But I thought it was Effie you wanted to know about.'

'Yes. Go on.'

'Well, I only know what the family legends say, because really she was rather mysterious. She went to Paris and worked there as an artist's model when she wasn't doing her own work. She was very poor, and it was the only way to make ends meet. And I think she fell in love with a French painter.'

'Did she marry him?'

'No. He died long before she did. Anyway after that she just worked harder and harder at her painting. She was a recluse and hardly ever went out. Cornelius tried to keep in touch, but his friends all thought she was peculiar.'

'The women in our family often are peculiar.'

'If you mean Grandma,' Mother said a bit sharply, 'that's quite different. Anyway, Effie went on living in France, getting more and more solitary. She loved cats. She lived in a tiny room with four of them and fed them better than she fed herself.

'Some people wanted to buy her work, but she painted very slowly and never delivered the pictures on time. I think she had difficulty with her eyes; she was gradually going blind in the last years. She died in – '

'Nineteen thirty-nine,' said Clare, looking at the diagram. 'That's the beginning of the Second World War.'

'Yes. Hitler had invaded France, and she'd lived through one war there already and must have thought she was too old to do it again. So she went to Dieppe with a crowd of refugees, probably trying to get a boat for England. I say probably, because she didn't tell anyone what she was going to do. And she collapsed in the street and died. No one knows where her grave is.'

'What about her cats?' asked Clare.

'Oh, she left enough money in her will to look after the cats.'

'Mum,' Jamie said, standing in the doorway clutching Persephone, 'I'm ravenous.'

'Well,' Mother said briskly, 'you'd better go out and buy some food. There's a little shop on the sea front. We'll need bread, milk, cereal, cat meat and something for our supper. Oh, and bin liners. We'll want plenty of them in the next few days.'

When Jamie had gone off, grumbling that it wasn't his job, she stood up.

'Come and look round.'

Clare followed her into the sitting-room.

'I'm sure people will want to buy this house. And that should solve our money problems. But before we let anyone see it, we must do a lot of cleaning.'

Clare saw that. The windows were filthy; the long curtains which had once been pale yellow were now pale grey and swathed in cobwebs. Dust was everywhere. Grandma apparently hadn't done any tidying up, just put things down and let them lie for months or years. There was also a vast pile of junk mail and copies of *The Times* dating back to the 1980s.

'It's a pity,' Mother said with a sigh. 'She used to be so houseproud.'

Clare sighed too. 'What are we going to do first?'

'The most important things. We'll find some sheets, make the beds and unpack.'

The sheets were old-fashioned white cotton ones, beginning to fray. They tidied a corner of Mother's and Jamie's rooms, but even that was difficult, because the newspapers and other rubbish took up most of the floor. After they'd unpacked they were so exhausted they didn't go out again. Even though it was summer, it was still very cold in the house that night.

Next morning the forecast threatened rain. Mother said there was just time for a good walk, so they put on their coats and went out. They went first through Clyne Gardens, near the old castle, then down to the front. It seemed strange to see miles and miles of sand, and nobody walking on it except a man and his dog. Mother told them that the waters of the bay had been polluted, years ago.

'We'll go swimming,' she said, 'when I can afford to take you.'

'Why does Mum always worry about money?' Clare asked Jamie as they went ahead together. 'We've got two houses now, haven't we – '

'God, you're so stupid, Earwig,' Jamie said scathingly.

'I'm not,' said Clare, hurt.

'Don't you see, twerp, Dad won't want to go on living in a bedsit for the rest of his life. Specially if he gets married again and has some more children.'

'I never thought of that.'

'Well, think now. If Gran hadn't died when she did, we'd probably have had to sell the house and go to an even smaller one. One of those poky little maisonettes in Milton Keynes. And I might have had to leave school and get a job. It's a good thing she died.'

'Jamie, that's a horrible thing to say!'

Jamie just shrugged.

Mother came up smiling. 'It's good to be here, isn't it?' Clare guessed she was glad to be back in Swansea because it was the town she'd grown up in. 'Even though they've done their best to ruin it, it's a beautiful coastline.'

'Mum, can Minnie come and stay with us when she gets back?' Minnie was in Minorca with her father and his girlfriend. 'I'd like to show her Wales.'

'If Minnie comes, I'm going,' Jamie said. He'd walked a bit away from them and was staring out gloomily over the bay.

'Well, that's all right! Mum, could Jamie go somewhere else and Minnie live with us and be my sister?'

'Oh, God,' Jamie said, 'how do you put up with her?'

It was the type of conversation they had every day.

By the time they got back to Grandma's house the weather had broken and they ate fish and chips on the kitchen table to the rising sound of rain.

Afterwards, Jamie announced that he was going out, put on his anorak, took a town map and some money and headed for the bus stop.

Clare looked after him enviously.

'Why can't I go too?'

'He's fifteen. You're only twelve. Besides, you don't know your way round yet, and the traffic is very heavy.'

'Aren't I ever to go out at all?'

Mother said, 'I promise we'll have one outing a day. Meanwhile, you can help me clean up, or watch TV, whichever you like.'

'I'll help,' Clare said virtuously.

She got a rag and some hot soapy water and set about washing the windows. It was hard work; the dirt came off very slowly. Mother was stuffing the bin liners with old papers and other rubbish, which she then dragged into the garden for the dustman to take away.

By the end of the afternoon they'd made a lot of progress, although they were both exhausted and had to vacuum up masses of black dust.

It wasn't until quite late, in the evening after Jamie had come back, that they found another picture by Effie.

CHAPTER 4

Mother found it, on top of Grandma's wardrobe. She said that she remembered it from years back, but Grandma had obviously got tired of looking at it and put it away in a plastic Marks and Spencer bag. But it hadn't come to much harm. It was a very small picture, framed and glazed, and beneath it was written:

'*Euphemia Price. A corner of the artist's room in Paris.*'

Clare took it to the window. It wasn't dark yet, and the pearly light revealed the painting clearly. In the foreground was a glass of carnations on a round table. The flowers were pink, but so pale they looked almost white; the light which fell on the table was white too and shone through a window without curtains which opened on to a shadowy street. There were more shadows in the room, framing the white rectangle of light and the carnations and glass.

'It's a bit colourless,' Jamie said, coming up behind her.

'No,' Clare said, still staring, 'it isn't.'

She was thinking it was the most lovely picture she had ever seen.

'Do wash your hands, Clare,' Mother said, 'I've made macaroni cheese.'

'Mum, can I have this picture in my room?'

'Why not?'

She propped the picture on the broad marble mantelpiece where she could see it when she was in bed. All evening, she kept going back to look at it, and in the night she switched on her lamp several times to make sure it was still there. She couldn't understand how anyone could ever have got tired of it.

Next morning when Jamie had gone out again and Mother was shopping, Clare settled down to ring her father. She knew that Mother was neurotic about her having long conversations on the phone in the daytime, but she thought she'd do it anyway.

Looking at herself in the big mirror on Grandma's walnut wardrobe, she thought how nice she looked in her crimson pyjamas and with her fair hair sticking out round her head like a halo. Nobody would think she was a person who used the phone when she wasn't supposed to. She had an angel face.

She heard the phone ringing far away in London and then it was answered by Dad's assistant, Vanessa.

'Can I speak to Mr Tom Drummond, please?'

'I'm afraid Mr Drummond's busy. We've only just opened the shop. Can I help?'

'It's Clare. Clare Drummond.'

'Oh. Well, just a minute, I'll call him.'

Her father's cheerful voice came on a moment later.

'Hello, sunshine, everything all right at your end?'

'You didn't come to see us before we left,' Clare said accusingly.

'I did suggest it, but your mother wasn't keen. Are you all well?'

'Yes, thank you.'

'And Persephone?'

'Yes. She's curled up at the end of Mum's bed.'

'Good. Now, what can I do for you at this hour in the morning?'

'Well, Dad, I was wondering, have you heard of Effie?'

'The sister of Cornelius. Yes. She was a painter too.'

'That's right. Are there any books about her in the shop?'

'I shouldn't think so. We might be able to find something on Cornelius, if that would do.'

'No, I'm only interested in Effie.'

'I see. Well, I'll look through the index and see if there's anything. But I wouldn't be too hopeful. She's not a famous name, exactly.'

'Thank you very much, Dad.'

'Is your mother there?'

'No, she popped out to the shop.'

'Well you'd better put that phone down before she catches you.' Clare giggled.

'Send me a postcard soon. Jamie, too.'

'Yes, Dad. Thank you.'

She hung up. She was fairly sure that if any book

on Effie existed, Dad would find it. He was good about that sort of thing.

Over the next few days Jamie grew more cheerful, if only because he spent hardly any time with Mother and her. What he did, Clare had no idea – probably window-shopping and taking long bus rides round Swansea. Meanwhile, they spent most of each day clearing Grandma's things. She'd help in the mornings when she was feeling fresh, then wander off to Clyne Gardens, where there were some amazing blue hydrangea bushes, and draw.

There were hundreds of books. Mother packed most of them into cardboard boxes, except an old photograph album covered with pink roses which she put on one side. Then there were Grandma's clothes and shoes. Most were falling apart and had to be thrown out too; the really old tattered ones went in the bin liner and the rest to Oxfam. They found one whole cupboard full of hats.

'Aren't they awful,' Mother said. 'No one will ever wear them again. Perhaps a theatre group could use them.'

Clare spent a happy hour trying them on in front of the big mirror. Amazing that people could ever have gone around with those things on their heads.

After lunch, they'd go on the bus to Swansea or wander along the front looking at the beautiful polluted bay. She and Mother were doing that one afternoon, a week after they'd arrived, when it began raining and they had to dash home. They tumbled inside, cold and breathless, and Mother put the kettle on while Clare flicked through the photograph album.

'Who's the old man with the white moustache?'

'That's my grandfather, Archibald,' Mother said, coming over to look. 'Cornelius and Effie's brother. I never knew him.'

'And he wasn't interested in painting?'

'No.'

Clare went on looking. They were all black and white photos, except some of the most recent. Her great-grandfather, Archie, and his wife who'd died young. His son Alan, in uniform; Clare realized with a shock that he looked a bit like Jamie. Grandma as a young woman, Grandma's husband. Mother as a little girl with pigtails, standing between her middle-aged parents. Mother and Dad's wedding photo. She didn't like to look at that.

Going back to the beginning, she found some very old brown tinted photographs. One of them was Cornelius as a young man; she'd seen enough pictures of him to be sure. He was very handsome, with a spade-shaped beard. She turned more pages. A small picture fell out of the book, and she picked it up.

A little girl in black Victorian mourning costume. She had a black hat and dress, her hair and eyes were dark and she was staring away from the camera. Her face looked serious and unhappy. The photograph was so old that it was covered with little black spots.

Clare turned it over. Somehow she already knew what would be written there in fading ink.

Effie, 1889.

'I've seen that,' Mother said, coming back into the room.'It was taken after her mother died.'

She began to spread the table for tea. Clare went on leafing through the album, but there were no more pictures of Effie.

'Thanks.'

She accepted a cup of tea and some blackcurrant jam.

'I've been meaning to ask,' Mother said after a moment, 'do you like living here?'

'Yes. It's much roomier than our house. I'll like it even better when it's clean. Mum, do you think, instead of selling it, we could keep it locked, and come here for the summer holidays?'

'We haven't got that sort of money, Clare. You see, we still need to pay off our mortgage – forty thousand pounds – and your father can't go on living in one room for ever. But I've had an idea – '

'Yes?'

'Well, how would you like it if we came to live here permanently?'

'What, instead of Milton Keynes?'

'Yes.'

Clare thought.

'Could Minnie come and stay with me?'

'I expect so.'

'And Dad?'

'He could move back into the house, or sell it and find a smaller place. Oh, you mean about seeing him. I'm sure that can be arranged. People think that we're a long way off, but it's only three hours from London by train.'

'But Mum, what about your job?'

'Maths teachers can always find jobs,' Mother said. 'But I think it would have to be a part-time job for the next few years, till I've got you and Jamie through school. I think I was trying to do too much, working full-time and being a single parent.'

Clare suddenly realized something.

'You really hate your job, don't you, Mum?'

'I suppose so.'

'Because Slogger hit you?'

'That was only the last straw. I've been getting very tired of that job for some time; the work is too hard and the hours are too long. A lot of my friends would get out if they could.'

Clare listened to the rain and tried to think. She understood that Mother was desperate to make a move, not only because Swansea was her native town and she'd been happy there, but also because she was sick of the old house and the old way of living. If she and Dad hadn't split up, of course it would have been different, but now she very much wanted a fresh start. And how did she feel, herself? A year ago she'd have said she didn't ever want to move, but now she, too, thought that she'd quite like it. She wasn't happy at home, perhaps she'd be happier here. It was certainly a much more interesting place.

She opened her mouth, but Mother was still talking.

'You see, Clare, things will be easier now we have a little more money. It's sad that this happened because of Grandma's death, but there it is. If we moved here I could forget about the mortgage, and I wouldn't have to look for a new job at once. What do you think?'

'About living here? Yes.'

'Are you quite sure?'

'Yes. I like it.'

'Good.' Mother sounded relieved. 'Well, I must talk to Jamie – '

'Don't bother. I heard.'

Jamie was standing by the door, which had been left open, so that they hadn't heard him come in. His anorak was dripping rain and his hair was wet so it looked darker than usual. His face was very white.

'Jamie,' Mother said with her usual calm, 'shut the door, and come and have some tea.'

Jamie kicked the door instead of shutting it.

'I heard you. Plotting behind my back, with her,' – he threw a contemptuous look at Clare – 'and of course you don't tell me, not till after you've decided!'

'Jamie,' Mother said, quietly but with a slight tremor in her voice, 'nothing is decided. I was going to talk it over – '

'Well, you should have f...ing well known!' Clare opened her mouth as he uttered the forbidden

36

word. '*I* don't want to come here. It's typical of you to plan it all without a word to me!'

'There's no need to be so – '

'*She'd* like it. She's so stupid she'll do anything you suggest. I'm not moving anywhere. You've already mucked up my whole life. And now you want to take me away from my school, and my friends, and Dad. Well I,' – Clare covered her ears again – 'f…ing won't come. You can't make me. If you sell the house, I'll go and live with Dad, or get a job.' His cheeks suddenly turning bright red, he shouted at the top of his voice, 'I'm grown up now and you can't push me around!'

Mother had taken a step towards him, but he pushed her away quite roughly and then ran out and locked himself in the bathroom. The pool of water from his anorak soaked into the worn carpet where he had stood.

CHAPTER 5

Clare wondered how she could ever have thought her run of bad luck was ending. Everything was miserable again, as normal.

She and Mother had both tried to reason with Jamie, but it was no good. He just kept on saying the same thing: he didn't mind if they kept the house for holidays but he refused to live there. When Clare asked him, tearfully, how he could do this to Mother when she so much wanted to get out of Milton Keynes he replied that he wasn't stopping her. Of course she could move if she liked but there was no way he'd come too.

'But then who would look after you?' Clare demanded.

'I can f…ing well look after myself.'

The really monstrously selfish thing about what Jamie was doing was that, as he'd often pointed out, he'd become a legal adult in two years and leave home anyway. He was supposed to be going on to Oxford or Cambridge; with his record, that would be no problem. So why was he refusing to fall in with their plans when it was for such a short time?

'There are some very good schools here,' Mother pleaded.

Jamie said, 'I don't care, I'm not going to them. *You* can live here if you like, with Earwig. I'll live with Dad.'

Mother said, '*No!*'

'He'll say yes, if I ask him,' Jamie flung over his shoulder and retreated into the next room to watch TV. It was raining so hard, all that day, that even he couldn't go out.

'Mum,' Clare said, when they were alone together, 'I think that might really be the best thing. He and Dad can stay in Milton Keynes, and you and I can move here. You're always saying you wish we didn't quarrel, and if we lived in different houses, we wouldn't.'

The way she felt about Jamie just now, she didn't care how far away he was.

Mother said, 'Clare, you don't understand.'

'We could go for holidays and see him.'

'That's nonsense, I wouldn't dream of leaving a boy of his age. Your father has no idea of how to look after him.'

It was Mother who was talking nonsense, Clare thought resentfully. She looked out of the window at the grey, foam-spattered sea. Dad might be useless around the house, but he was basically a sensible person and he was very fond of Jamie. The real reason, of course, was that Mother couldn't bear to let him go.

Probably she preferred him to her. People did prefer boys, she'd noticed. So because of Jamie, they'd have to sell this lovely house and go back to Milton Keynes which she hadn't liked ever since her parents split up. It was surprising how fiercely she wanted to stay here when, until yesterday, she'd never even thought of it. Perhaps, although that seemed very strange, it had something to do with Effie. Something fascinated her in the thought of that little girl in deep mourning, living in these rooms and walking on Swansea sands more that a hundred years ago. Perhaps it was because Effie had been good at painting and she, Clare, was also good at it. But people would laugh if she ever said such a thing out loud.

Jamie was still in a temper, they could tell from his pale cheeks and swollen eyes. He hardly spoke to either of them, though he obeyed when Mother asked him to move the heavy dustbins. She was keeping herself busy scrubbing the kitchen. It was filthy – floor, sink, surfaces, pans and cutlery – because hardly anything had been done in the last years of Grandma's life.

Clare played with Persephone until bedtime, and that was the end of the first full day after the row.

She lay in bed for a while, staring through the fading light at Effie's ghostly carnations, until at last the window clouded over and she slept. But she kept half-waking up; someone was playing a radio on the front. She dreamed that she was running down a lot of dark corridors looking for her parents and not finding them. Then she picked up the wedding photograph, and it had turned brown.

Then she woke up properly.

It was quite dark, but looking through the curtains she could see the lights of Swansea in the distance.

She jumped out of bed, thrust her arms into her dressing-gown, and went out to raid the fridge.

Groping past Effie's picture, which gazed at her serenely, she went downstairs and saw a light under the sitting-room door. Mother was by the gas fire looking at some papers.

'Clare! Have you just woken up?'

'Yes, What's the time?'

'Quarter to midnight.'

'Can I have some cocoa and biscuits, please?'

'Yes.' Mother got up. 'I think I'm hungry too. Sit by the fire and keep warm.'

While she was out of the room, Clare sneaked a look at the papers which lay on a little table by her chair. Bills.

'Are we not going to live here, then?' she asked when Mother came back with a tray.

Mother sighed. 'Not without Jamie.'

'Couldn't you *make* him come?'

'I think a court would listen to a boy of that age, if he wanted to be with his father. Anyway, I'm not going to take the risk.'

'It isn't fair that you should have to go back to that job, when you hate it.'

'Oh –' Mother said, with a smile that didn't reach her eyes. 'My mother used to say, "it isn't fair but it's life".'

Clare held the mug in her hands, waiting for it to cool.

'How much money have we got, Mum?'

'A bit more than before, not as much as we need. I've decided to sell the Cornelius picture.'

'That must be worth about a million pounds.'

'I'm afraid not.'

'Why ever not? He's famous, isn't he?'

'It ought to have been sold thirty years ago. Apparently Cornelius is nothing like as popular as he used to be. The art experts have decided he wasn't a genius, after all.'

This was so extraordinary that Clare was struck dumb.

'You don't mind letting it go, do you, Clare?'

'No,' Clare said slowly, 'as long as you don't sell Effie's pictures too.'

'Oh, I shouldn't think anyone would want them.'

The fire crackled. Clare sipped the scalding cocoa.

'You see,' Mother went on after a short silence, 'Jamie is going into the sixth form and he'll be working very hard for A levels. I must keep a home together for him for another two years. After that, you and I can go wherever we like.'

'To this house?'

'I don't know.'

'It's a shame if you have to sell it, after a hundred years.' Her eyes fell on the album with its pink, rose-decorated cover and that reminded her of something. 'Did Grandma live here all her life?'

'Yes, she did. You see, her mother died and she had to take over as her father's housekeeper. She had a rather sad life, because her brother, Alan, died in the war. It was a great waste; he's said to have been very clever.'

42

Like Jamie, Clare thought, but didn't say.

'And then Archibald – her father – became even more grouchy than he already was. I don't think he ever got over his son being killed. So my poor mother never met any young men or went anywhere except to church until after he died. She was forty when she did get married, which is why I'm an only child. They called me Anne as it was the nearest they could get to Alan.'

'He was the important one, wasn't he? The boy.'

'What do you mean?'

Clare changed the subject.

'I wouldn't have done what she did, living with a grouchy old man and waiting on him. Why didn't she just walk out?'

'Well, Clare, women expected to stay with their families in those days, and your grandmother had – I suppose you'd call them old-fashioned ideas. I'm glad she never knew I was getting a divorce. She'd have been horrified.'

The words burst out before Clare could stop them.

'Mum, why did you do it? I've never understood. Dad is such a nice man!'

For a second she thought Mother wasn't going to answer. Then she said, 'It's not so simple Clare. I never said your father wasn't a nice man. I just said I couldn't live with him.'

'But *why*?'

'We kept quarrelling.'

43

'That isn't true. You never quarrelled at all, not till about two years ago!'

She was sure of that. For most of her life, there had been no quarrels.

'I don't know if you can understand, Clare – ' Mother began.

'I can. A lot of my friends are divorced, I mean their parents are.'

'Yes. Well, some of what you say is true. I married your father expecting it to last and for a long time we were very happy. But then he began to behave in a way I couldn't stand.'

'Had he got a mistress?' She'd learned that word in connection with Cornelius, who had had several.

'Oh, no. No, Tom has plenty of faults, but not that one. The trouble began when he lost his job.' Clare tried to remember that time; she knew her parents had been badly worried but the details were hazy. 'It did things to him.'

'What?'

'He got very depressed. He was unemployed for a year, and I had to go back to teaching, which I'd resisted because I thought you needed me at home. It hurt Dad, I think, that I was the breadwinner instead of him.'

Her face was still calm but her small hands were clenching and unclenching.

'Well – we started to fight about quite unimportant things. I'm sure you remember. In the end he found the job he's got now and I hoped things would improve. Only it meant commuting to London so

44

we hardly ever saw him. I considered giving up my own job, but I didn't dare.'

'Jamie thinks that all the trouble started with you going back to work.'

'Jamie believes what he wants to believe. I had no choice. I know you think I'm mean, worrying about phone bills and so on, but it's because we've been really hard up.'

'Sorry, Mum.'

'Never mind. It won't be so bad in future. Well, there isn't much more to tell. I felt I was being pulled in all directions, worrying about my job, looking after you children, cleaning and cooking and trying to hold the family together. And then Grandma was going downhill, and Dad was no help at all. Something had to break, and in the end it was our marriage.'

'You mean he walked out?'

She'd never really forgiven him for that.

'No. I asked him to go.'

'Why? I wish you hadn't.'

'It was simpler,' her mother said in an exhausted voice. 'There were no more quarrels. As a matter of fact, Dad and I get on much better since we split up. That doesn't mean that it was easy; it was very painful. Whatever you do, Clare, take your time before you get married – don't rush into anything.'

'I won't,' Clare said. 'I don't think I'll ever get married at all.'

CHAPTER 6

Effie hadn't got married. Effie had devoted herself to painting, even though she'd been in love with the mysterious Frenchman, and Clare thought she'd probably had quite an interesting life. True, she wasn't famous, like Cornelius – but as she drifted off, she remembered that even Cornelius wasn't very famous now.

She woke up late next morning, having slept in after her long talk with Mother. She felt hot and headachey and aware that something was wrong, though she didn't know what. She heard the sound of heavy rain outside and then realized what had woken her. The telephone.

She got up and padded downstairs to the sitting-room. Mother was listening and she could hear her father's unmistakable booming tones at the other end.

'Children all right, Anne?'

'Yes, thank you.'

'And you?'

'Fine.'

'Good. Well, I'm just giving you a buzz to say that I'll be in Wales the second week in August. I've got an interview at the Student Bookshop.'

'That's nice,' Mother said coolly.

'Yes. So I thought I'd stop over a couple of nights, have a look round and see you.'

'Would you like a bed?'

'That's very good of you, Anne,' – Dad sounded a bit embarrassed – 'but actually, Vanessa's going to drive me down and put me up. She's got a married sister in Cardiff.'

'I see. Well, Tom, I hope it works out.'

'So do I. I'll wear a leek in my buttonhole. Look forward to seeing you.'

Mother put the phone down.

When Jamie got up, about half-past ten, and heard that his father was coming, he looked more cheerful than he had for days. They ate a late breakfast. The rain had finally stopped, and a pale watery sun was shining brilliantly over the sea.

'Mum,' Clare asked, 'what did Dad mean about wearing a leek?'

Mother said, 'It means he may have a slightly better chance of getting the job because he's Welsh. I hope he will; he never did like living in the Home Counties.'

'That's ridiculous,' Jamie said. '*I'm* glad I'm English.'

'You're not, Jamie. Mum and Dad are both Welsh, so you are too.'

'Shut up, Earwig, no one cares what you think.'

'Stop brawling, please,' Mother said. 'Well, we must go out while the fine weather lasts. I think I've done enough cleaning! Jamie, what do you want to do today?'

'Play golf somewhere.'

'What about me?' asked Clare.

Mother said, 'I'll take you to the Fruitmarket Gallery. They've got several paintings by Cornelius.'

Clare felt much more cheerful as they walked to the bus stop in the sunshine, which she hadn't seen for days. There were gulls wheeling overhead and a lot of people walking about dressed for summer. The last forty-eight hours seemed like a bad dream.

There was just one thing nagging at the back of her mind, and that was Vanessa. She'd never met her, but Dad had said something about her being quite a young woman and having had a disastrous boyfriend. But she was probably just being kind, giving Dad a lift and a room.

The gallery was in a converted warehouse in Swansea. They went into a big white room decorated with art posters.

Mother said, 'I wonder if old Mr Lloyd Roberts still works here. I knew him years ago. Yes, there he is behind the desk.'

A minute later they were shaking hands with an elderly gentleman whose eyes behind his silver spectacles lit up on seeing Mother.

'Well, this *is* a pleasant surprise. Miss Anne Llewellyn – I'm afraid I've forgotten your married name?'

'Mrs Drummond. And this is my little girl, Clare.'

'Delighted to meet you, Miss Clare,' Mr Lloyd Roberts said. 'Although I would have thought your mother was too young and pretty to have a daughter your age.'

'I've got a boy, too,' Mother said, 'who's taller than I am.'

'Indeed? I wonder if he'll be a painter when he grows up. Rebecca,' he added to the girl behind the desk, 'this lady is a close relation of Cornelius Price.'

Clare beamed. This was fame.

'A great man, a very great man. We're very proud of him in Swansea. I don't know if you remember him, Miss Anne?'

'Just about,' Mother said.

'I last saw him around the time of his eightieth birthday. He lived on the English side of the border, as you know, but he'd look in whenever he was here. A wonderful old gentleman, interested in everything. So you'll be wanting to show the little girl his pictures?'

'Excuse me,' Clare said.

'Yes, my dear?'

'Have you got any pictures by Effie?'

'Euphemia? Well, we have a small self-portrait in our reserve collection, but I would have to fetch the key. Would you like to see it?'

'Yes, please.'

'Look after the desk, Rebecca,' Mr Lloyd Roberts said, 'while we take a little tour. But first you'll want to see our Cornelius Prices.'

They walked into a big room where several pictures were hanging. Three of them were by Cornelius: a bowl of cornflowers, a nude and a portrait of Lord Someone.

'Beautiful,' Mother said, and 'Aren't they!' Mr Lloyd Roberts echoed reverently.

They went down some stairs, along a little passage and then Mr Lloyd Roberts unlocked a door. Inside were several pictures in stacks.

'There she is,' Mr Lloyd Roberts said, picking out a very small one and turning it to the light. 'That's Euphemia.'

Clare found herself looking for the first time at the grown-up Effie. It was quite a young woman that she saw, dark hair scraped back in the style of the early twentieth century, and wearing a high blouse the colour of red sealing-wax. Her face looked – Clare searched for the right word and could find only one – prim. She also realized, and this surprised her very much, that she had a distinct look of Mother.

But that wasn't so strange, after all. The same faces went on and on in families through the generations.

'It's beautiful,' she said.

'Yes,' Mr Lloyd Roberts agreed. 'She had a little bit of her brother's talent.'

'Why do you keep it locked up?'

'Well, my dear, we've got far more pictures than we can show, so we hang only the best ones. But next year we're holding an exhibition on Cornelius and his circle, so we'll bring her into the light briefly.'

Clare took a last look at the picture before it was put back and the store-room relocked. Then they talked some more to Mr Lloyd Roberts, walked around the gallery, and ended up in the tea rooms. Clare bought a postcard (by Cornelius, of course) to send Dad.

'I liked that picture, Mum, didn't you?'

'Cornelius?'

'No, Effie.'

'You know me,' Mother said neutrally. 'I've never claimed to be an art expert.'

Clare sighed.

'I wish I knew more about Effie, just the same.'

'You could probably find something in the biography of Cornelius. I'll see if we've got one – no, we haven't, but we'll try the public library.'

After Clare had finished her Coke they went there. Mother got tickets, and they both chose some books – including, from the adult section, a huge, fat, black volume called *The Life of Cornelius Price*.

'I can't read all that,' Clare said in horror.

'You don't have to,' Mother smiled. 'Just look in the index for Effie's name.'

Then they went round the market, and bought bread and fresh fish and some sweet seedless grapes for the weekend. They were both exhausted when they got back.

'That's all I'm going to do today!' Mother said.

But already they had done a great deal. Grandma's house was clean, and there was space to move around. The rubbish had been thrown out and the good jumble sorted. You could see now what a nice house it would be if it was decorated and the aged carpets and curtains renewed. Clare wandered into her bedroom.

She could do things with this room, she thought, if they ever moved here. She'd have her furry animals, and her pink curtains, and each morning she could jump out of bed and look at the sea. But she'd keep the little round mirror and Effie's painting. Even if things were never going to happen, it was nice to plan them in your mind.

Jamie came back from his golf in a fairly good mood and they had tea. In the evening, Clare tucked up in bed with Persephone on the blanket and began reading *The Life of Cornelius Price*.

CHAPTER 7

The book was by somebody called Marcus Richards and it was seven hundred pages long. First, Clare looked at the photographs. There was Cornelius as a young man, wearing a painter's smock and looking spectacularly handsome, and Cornelius as an old man with a flowing white beard. There were his three wives, and some other women, and his children dressed in the peculiar clothes people wore at the turn of the century. And, of course, his best-known paintings in black and white.

No pictures of Effie. Clare checked the index and found a list of page numbers after her name, which she'd look up. But to begin with she read the first chapter, about how Cornelius had grown up in this house a few miles' drive from Victorian Swansea. No cars then, they'd have gone to town in a horse-drawn cab. How he and his sister, Effie, had been very close in those days, and how their brother Archibald had been born when they were eight and nine. If he hadn't been, Clare thought, she wouldn't be here.

Then it told how Cornelius's mother had died, and how he and Effie had gone down with paper and pencil to the beach every day, getting steadily more obsessed with drawing. They hadn't had much time for baby Archie, it seemed. And how he had gone away to study art in London, Effie following.

The next bit was all about his first wife, May, who'd died, and his mistress, Violet. Clare wrinkled her nose at some of the details. Really he had been a rather disgusting old man.

There wasn't much about Effie, except a stray line here and there. About a hundred pages on, the book said:

'After his wife died, Cornelius hoped that Effie would look after the four children, but she remained in Paris, painting.'

Good for Effie, Clare thought. She was sure Cornelius would have found some other woman to move in with him. And she was quite right, he had. She flicked over more pages. Cornelius with wife number two, Cornelius and his very young third wife, Cornelius the grand old man of British painting –

And she mustn't go to sleep, because here was another bit about Effie.

'The last meeting between Cornelius and his sister was in August 1938 when Effie briefly crossed the Channel. She had grown more and more eccentric over the years. Cornelius urged her to stay in England, to escape the threat of war, but she refused, saying she had to get back to her cats. She left with him a box of her exquisite small sketches.'

She went on a few more pages and came to the account of Effie's death in Dieppe as Hitler's army swept through France. The last sentence which interested her read:

'In his generous way, Cornelius said, "After a

hundred years, I shall be remembered mainly as the brother of Euphemia Price".'

Clare went to sleep with her lamp still on.

Next morning, Sunday, she was woken by church bells. She realized that the heavy book was still on her pillow and that she'd been too tired to read properly last night. But her mind must have been working in her sleep, because one thing was clear to her. Effie's drawings hadn't been lost in the war, like so much else. Probably someone in the family had them still.

She got up, put on her dressing-gown and wandered into the kitchen where her mother was breaking eggs.

'Hello, Mum.'

'How did you get on with the book?' Mother asked. 'It put you to sleep, did it?'

'Yes, it was very dull. Mother,' – Clare sat down at the table and helped herself to orange juice – 'you knew Cornelius, didn't you?'

'Hardly at all. I was only a child when he died. He used to pat my head and say I looked like a snowdrop.'

'What did you think of him?'

'Oh, we all thought he was a very distinguished old man.'

The bells were clanging steadily, the sun creeping all over the room.

'It's very odd,' Clare said. 'Everybody thinks that Cornelius was the genius of the family, but I like Effie much better. Am I mad?'

'Not at all,' Mother said. She began to slice a loaf. 'You see, Clare, if there's a problem in maths it has only one answer. The others simply aren't true. But with a poem, or a painting, you can decide for yourself what you like.'

'I still don't understand why Cornelius is famous and she isn't.'

'Oh,' Mother said, 'I don't know anything about art, but I can understand that.'

'Go on.'

'Well, Cornelius was living in London, going about and making friends with other painters who all said nice things about each other's work. And besides, he was the sort of man who gets noticed. He had a lot of personality, even in old age. Whereas Effie lived very quietly, hardly met anyone and never tried to become famous. And from what I've heard, she was so shy people hardly knew she was there.'

'I wish I could meet somebody who knew her. Is there anyone left?'

'Let's think,' said Mother. 'Grandma knew her, but it's too late to ask. Cornelius's children are all dead. Except his youngest daughter, Ruby. She's retired now and living in Brighton. She might remember.'

Ruby. She had a vague impression of a large lady with a cheerful laugh and stylish white hair.

'Can I ring her up?'

Because Ruby might know something about that box of drawings which Effie had brought from France half a century ago. It was worth asking.

'Of course. Here's my address book.'

But at that moment Jamie came in, rubbing his eyes and demanding to be fed, so Clare didn't make the call. She suspected that Jamie would laugh if he knew how interested she was getting in Effie.

That day they packed a picnic lunch and went by bus to Rhosili. It took a long time, but it was worth it when they had climbed down to the beach. Jamie swam miles out and gambolled about like a porpoise while Clare splashed inexpertly nearer the land. Afterwards they towelled themselves and ate sausage rolls and drank pop and Clare climbed on to the Worm's Head, watching the waves chase each other like white horses around the enormous curve of bay.

Some day she'd paint this. She'd come back with her equipment and put down the golden light, the gulls and the transparent sea. She'd get it down to two or three colours, blue, white, yellow, and then it wouldn't be this particular beach but anywhere the land and sea met.

She came back with a jolt to reality. In a few weeks they'd be gone, and perhaps she'd never be able to come back, if they sold Grandma's house. It was awful to think of.

Once they were home, after a long bus ride, Mother made some hot chocolate and Jamie shut himself in the bathroom to get the salt out of his hair. He didn't seem likely to come out for a while, so Clare decided it was safe to phone Cornelius's daughter Ruby. Mrs Earl.

'She's very nice,' Mother assured her, 'so don't be shy.'

Clare dialled the number.

'Hello.'

'Hello,' Clare said a bit nervously, 'this is Clare Drummond.'

'Oh, yes. Anne's daughter. We've met before, Clare. How's your nice brother Jamie?'

'All right,' Clare said rather coldly.

'And your parents?'

'They've split up.'

'Oh dear. Stupid question.'

She had a nice voice, quite jolly and understanding.

'I expect you're wondering why I've rung you. Well, my grandmother died a couple of months ago – '

'I knew her.'

'– and me and Mum and Jamie are here in Swansea to tidy the house. While I was here I got interested in Effie – '

'So you're in Wales, Clare. How exciting. I haven't been there for years, but my father grew up in that house. Is it going to be sold, I wonder? Sorry, you were asking me about Effie.'

'Yes. You see, I've heard that Effie gave Cornelius, I mean your dad, a box of her drawings the last time she saw him. Have you still got them, please?'

She paused breathlessly. She felt she'd almost got her hands on them already.

'I'm afraid not,' Ruby's voice said. 'I never heard about any box of drawings.'

CHAPTER 8

For a moment, Clare was too bitterly disappointed to speak. She'd been so sure that Cornelius would have looked after those drawings, that she could get hold of them almost straight away. And now they were lost, probably destroyed. Had been lost for fifty years.

'It's very strange,' Ruby went on, 'but you're the second person who's rung me about Effie this year. There was a young woman from Cardiff, Olwen somebody, who came all the way to Brighton to see my two Euphemia Prices.'

Clare felt better.

'You've got two of Effie's pictures in your house?'

'Yes. One of a girl in a blue shawl, and a still life of strawberries. Olwen said she'd tried to contact your grandmother, but she wouldn't let her in.'

'I'm afraid Grandma got rather odd in her last years. Perhaps I can tell this person that she can come now.'

'Let me see. Her name is Olwen Hughes, and this is her number.'

Clare copied it on the telephone pad.

'Well, Clare, I gather you've fallen in love with Effie's paintings. I'm not surprised. She was a very interesting woman, not as good as Cornelius perhaps but she had definite talent. What else can I tell you?'

'Did you know her? Effie?'

'Oh, yes.'

'What sort of person was she?'

'Difficult to say because she hardly ever spoke. She was small, and dressed in black, and kept a lot of cats which she was very fond of. You see I was only a child in the 1930s – how old are you by the way, Clare?'

'Twelve.'

'Well, I was younger than that when Effie died. Father took us to Paris one year and I visited her wretched little studio. Even then I could see that she didn't look after herself properly. We went round an exhibition of Picasso's drawings and – oh, dear, it was very funny!'

Her laugh echoed over the phone.

'What did Effie do?'

'Well, my mother said weren't they wonderful, and Effie said – we could hardly hear her, she had a very quiet voice – "These are very good, but I prefer my own".'

Clare knew the feeling.

'And was that the last time you saw her?'

'No. One more time. She did come to England, as you said, the year before the war. I had a marvellous childhood, you know, Clare. All the great painters used to stay with us – Stanley Spencer, Dame Laura Knight. But now I think of it, Effie never came to our house in Sussex. Let me see.'

Clare waited breathlessly.

'Father used to go to the Gower peninsula every

summer to paint. Yes, we were at our little cottage and Effie spent a few days in Archie's house. We had Sunday lunch there. Your grandmother did the cooking, she was quite a young girl. And I met her brother Alan, who died. Such a nice-looking boy. We were talking about Hitler, I remember. Yes, it would have been the summer of 1938.'

'So if Effie gave Cornelius her drawings then – '

'It was in Swansea,' Ruby said firmly. 'So if I were you, I'd look first in your grandmother's house.'

Mother had listened to all this with a slightly quizzical expression but when Clare poured out the story she shook her head.

'I've turned out every drawer in the entire house, and looked at everything, and I'm perfectly certain that Effie's drawings aren't here. You'll just have to think of somewhere else.'

'Couldn't I ask this person, Marcus someone, who wrote the biography?'

'No, you can't , because he's dead.'

They stared at each other and then had the same idea at the same moment.

'Of course, I haven't been in the loft yet – '

'The loft!' Clare shrieked.

'Oh, no!' Mother groaned. 'I wasn't going to start on that till I felt stronger. There's all sorts of old rubbish lying about. Grandma didn't touch it for decades.'

'I'll do it, Mum. Just let me go up there and I'll do all the work.'

'I might have known!'

While Mother fetched a step-ladder Clare looked around the big sitting-room, which was growing shadowy, and thought of the family party which had gathered there that Sunday in August 1938, all of them dead now, except one. The furnishings that looked so tatty would have been new and fresh, and they would have sat round the oval mahogany table and afterwards broken up into little groups. Archibald, the respectable middle-aged lawyer, probably not approving much of his artist brother and sister. Grandma, a young woman then, thin and bony and terribly overworked. And her brother Alan, who'd looked like Jamie, a schoolboy of sixteen.

And Cornelius, who would have done most of the talking. And his young wife in arty floating clothes and the little girl, Ruby. And Effie, who would certainly not have said much.

Grandma would have given them coffee in the small cups with pale purple daisies, which they'd got still. And Cornelius might have said, 'Well, Effie, if you insist on going back to France, leave your drawings with me.' Only he might have forgotten to take them after all, he was that sort of man. He'd have gone home, leaving them in Archie's house, and Archie would have put them away somewhere, meaning to hand them over when they next met. But then the war had come, and for years people had thought of nothing else. Effie was dead and couldn't ask for her drawings, and a deeply depressed Archie probably hadn't even thought about them. Until, at some stage, they'd been put in the loft, and lain there for the best part of fifty years.

Yes, that was how it must have happened.

'You don't think that Grandma might have thrown them out?' she said, suddenly struck by a horrible thought as Mother dragged the step-ladder upstairs.

'I shouldn't think so,' Mother said, placing it carefully under the trapdoor. 'Grandma wasn't interested in art, but she knew that other people were.'

She opened the door, got out her torch and flashed it into the loft. Climbing up, she groped around a bit and then switched on a weak light.

'Here you are. But put on my overall; you'll get filthy.'

'Is the loft really full of stuff?'

'Yes.'

She came down. Clare rolled up her sleeves and got into the blue overall, then went up the ladder.

Cobwebs grazed her cheek. She saw a large, dimly lit room, crammed with every sort of lumber. Old pieces of furniture which her grandparents couldn't quite bring themselves to part with, cardboard boxes, cases, trunks. Golf clubs – she must tell Jamie – her grandfather's fishing tackle, a very ancient hip-bath. Plastic bags stuffed full; Grandma had obviously been the sort who threw nothing away. And there was fluff, grey fluff every-where.

'It's spooky!' she shouted down to Mother.

'You wanted to go there,' Mother said.

Clare decided to do the job systematically. Having felt the plastic bags, and made sure that there was nothing in them but clothes, she moved on to the cardboard boxes. She was very interested in one which contained some framed pictures, but they were obviously not by Effie, just some views of Swansea and the bay that even she could see weren't much good. Piles of women's magazines from the 1950s. A thick brown envelope, labelled *Alan's letters*. Some very ugly old china ornaments. What a shame she hadn't given this stuff away!

She worked through the boxes, then the suitcases and an enormous old-fashioned trunk, but found only more clothes. It began to worry her. After all, she had only been guessing; perhaps Effie's drawings had been burned or thrown out for rubbish many years ago. Then her eye fell on a little delicate-looking chest of drawers which stood inconspicuously against one wall, behind a sagging armchair.

'Of course!'

She went over and pulled open the lowest drawer, leaving handprints on the dusty surface as she did so.

Old newspaper lined it. There was a flat, rectangular cardboard box inside.

Effie's drawings

Grandma had written it in pencil on the lid.

'I've got them! I found them! I'm brilliant!'

Clare was almost crowing with delight as she

spread her drawings out on the big table where the Price family had had lunch together, more than fifty years ago.

There was dust in her hair, in her shoes, on everything. Mother had made her wash her hands before she was allowed to touch them. She was looking quite interested, Clare thought, although she'd never admit it, of course.

There were seven drawings on different-sized sheets of paper, none bigger than A4. Three of a grey and white cat, one coloured and the rest done in pencil. One of a cup and teapot, another of redcurrants in a glass bowl. The last two were of a little sharp-faced girl in a winter coat and hat. One was in charcoal, the other in bottle-green and lemon-yellow.

'I like this best,' Clare gloated.

'Yes.' Mother gazed down at them thoughtfully. 'They're not bad.'

'Why do you think all her pictures are so tiny?'

'Probably because she couldn't afford large canvasses. She'd just carry a sketch pad round with her and draw when she found something interesting.'

Of course, Clare thought, a small picture needn't be any worse than a large one. She looked again at the little girl in the dark green coat and decided she'd keep it in her bedroom with the other picture. How lovely, how utterly lovely. How could anyone think that Effie wasn't good?

CHAPTER 9

Jamie stood in front of the bathroom mirror, studying his face as he'd done ever since he got out of bed fifteen minutes ago. First he got a comb and adjusted his parting, then he dabbed his hair with water, then he made a slight change to his parting again. Fidgeting behind him, trying to get a corner of the mirror for herself, Clare grew exasperated.

'It's all right, Jamie, you haven't got any more spots in the night.'

'Shut up,' Jamie said automatically.

'Can you move a bit, please? I want to put my slides in.'

'You needn't bother,' Jamie answered, 'you'll still look stupid. All you think about is putting silly little bits of plastic in your hair, or that awful Effie.'

For it had been impossible to stop Jamie finding out about her interest in Effie, after he'd seen her poring over her drawings last night. And he had been teasing her ruthlessly ever since.

'Effie is *not* awful.'

'Why are you so fascinated by her? She's dead, isn't she? She's been dead for a hundred years.'

'Fifty years actually.'

'It's all the same. Cornelius was a much better painter than she was. Personally,' Jamie said, 'I can't stand his stuff and I think he was a complete bore, but at least he got famous and made loads of money. Effie was no good at anything.'

'That's not true.'

'It is. If she was as good as you say, why isn't she famous, like Cornelius? Everyone knows that women can't paint.'

'I can paint and you can't!'

'Children,' Mother said resignedly, coming to the bathroom door, 'for heaven's sake stop squabbling! I'm fed up with it. And come and eat your pancakes, before they're cold.'

There was a mad rush to the kitchen.

'Mum,' Jamie said, when he'd put away the pancakes and about a pint of yogurt, 'are you going to sell the Cornelius picture?'

'I think so, Jamie.'

'Good. Then maybe we'll have enough money to keep this house for holidays?'

'I don't know. We'll have to see.'

Perhaps, Clare thought, Mother and I can really come and live here. If not now, then in two years' time. And tonight I'll ring this person, Olwen. She was still feeling extremely pleased with herself.

Something dropped through the letter-box. Jamie went to the door and brought back a large envelope.

'A letter from Dad!' Clare shrieked.

'Don't be stupid, Earwig, he's only sending on our mail.'

Mother had opened the envelope and brought out a handful of letters. Each of the children had a card from friends who'd gone abroad. Clare's was from Minnie and read, 'Very nice here but I've got sunburn and Dad and Sharon keep fighting. Perhaps they'll split up!!! Today I had a pineapple ice-cream. Let me know if I can come to Wales XXXX Minnie.'

'Has Dad written to you, Mum?' Jamie asked.

'Yes. Just a note to say that everything at home is fine and he'll see us on Friday, when he has his interview.'

'Is he bringing Vanessa?' Clare blurted out, and then wished she hadn't.

'He doesn't say so,' Mother said coolly, 'but I believe they're driving down together.'

Jamie muttered, 'Bitch.'

'Jamie,' Mother said, 'I've told you, I don't want to hear that word.'

'Sorry.'

'And since your father is not married to me now, there's no reason why he shouldn't see other people.'

'He is married to you.'

'Not for much longer. Anyway, I doubt if Vanessa is anything more than his assistant.'

Jamie looked cynical but didn't reply.

Mother kept herself busy all that day, either going out to shop or bringing down more armfuls of stuff from the loft. As she said, whether or not the house was sold, they might as well get it in good shape. Clare drew some horses.

As soon as six o'clock struck she phoned the number which Ruby had given her and asked to speak to Olwen Hughes. It seemed to be a communal phone because it took some time before she was found. Her voice was rather breathless with a North Wales accent.

'Are you interested in Effie?' Clare demanded.

'Effie *Price*?'

'Yes. I'm her great-great-niece.'

'Who is that speaking, please?'

'Clare Drummond. I'm staying in Swansea in my grandmother's house, and I heard you'd come to see Gran and she wouldn't let you in, but now she's dead.'

'Oh, I see.' The voice sounded more breathless than ever. 'Sorry, Clare, this is all quite a surprise to me. I didn't know the old lady had died. You're right, I am very interested in Effie. Tell me, have you got any of her work?'

'Yes,' Clare said triumphantly, 'two oil paintings, and seven little drawings, which I only found in the loft yesterday.'

'That's wonderful!'

She sounded genuinely thrilled.

'Would you like to come here and see them? My mother will give you tea.'

'That's very kind. Let's see, I'm working in a bakery just now – looking for a real job – but I could come over on Saturday afternoon. Will you be there?'

'Course I will. I'd like to talk about Effie, nobody else is interested in her.'

'Oh, that's going to change. See you in five days, then.'

They fixed the details and Clare put down the

phone, glowing. Come the weekend, she'd be seeing this girl who knew all about Effie, and seeing Dad, too.

The next few days passed slowly. Clare went to the Glynn Vivian Art Gallery with her mother and saw a huge painting by Cornelius Price. It was a rainy day, and she very much enjoyed wandering around and looking up at the glowing pictures. Quite a few were better than the one by Cornelius, she thought.

As for Jamie, they hardly saw him, because he was always out.

On Thursday Dad phoned to tell them he'd be calling at tea-time next day. The house was looking good now and smelling of lavender polish. On Friday morning they went out and bought an iced orange cake and a packet of China tea and a bunch of sweet peas for the table. Then they made cucumber sandwiches and put out Grandma's best china. Clare guessed that Mother was thinking the same as her; if Vanessa was coming, they weren't going to be shamed.

She hoped she wouldn't come, though.

Four o'clock struck. Jamie hurried back and put on a fresh shirt. Then they heard a car draw up, the bell rang and they opened the door to let in Dad and, behind him, Vanessa.

Clare had always thought her father was extremely handsome. He was just forty, having had a birthday last month, but he didn't look middle-aged. In fact he looked a bit like a schoolboy, with rumpled fair hair and bright blue eyes like hers. He was a big man, much taller than Mother.

Vanessa, Clare calculated, was about fifteen years younger. She had blonde hair, wore a lot of make-up and was stylishly dressed in white and red. As she came forward and said some polite words Clare shot a glance from her to Mother. She looked nice, she always did, but she was a lot older than Vanessa and definitely not so glamorous. She was a bit quieter than usual, perhaps, but Vanessa talked quite enough for two.

Dad had brought them presents. A cassette for Jamie and a box of good pastels for her. They sat round the mahogany table having tea, and Clare answered Vanessa's questions about her school while she tried to listen to the conversation on her other side, between Mother and Dad.

'How was your interview, Tom?'

'Fine. I really think they're interested. And I'd be much happier working here than in London with Mr Big.' Mr Big was his boss. 'Did I tell you they've asked me to look in again tomorrow morning?'

'What for?'

'Just to talk. And after that I thought I'd take the children out. To the zoo, perhaps.'

'Clare can't go,' Mother said, 'she's meeting a friend from Cardiff.'

'Who's that, Clare?' Vanessa enquired sweetly.

'Oh, just a person,' Clare said. No way was she going to tell this woman anything about Effie.

'Well, Jamie, then,' said Dad.

'I'm too old for the zoo,' Jamie said morosely.

'Okay, we'll do a film or whatever you like. I'll pick you up after lunch. Is that all right?'

Jamie mumbled something.

'What a beautiful house, Anne,' Vanessa said in a bright voice. 'Such a good view of the bay. You *are* lucky.'

'What are you going to do about the house, Anne?' Dad asked.

Mother said, 'Sell it, probably.' Clare had the feeling that she would have liked to talk to him, about money and about where they were going to live, but couldn't with Vanessa listening. She thought it was extraordinary that anyone could be so tactless. When they'd finished tea, and Dad was trying to start a conversation with Jamie, she hung around, asking him where he wanted to go tomorrow, from which Clare deduced that she meant to go too. How awful! Just as well that she had an excuse to stay away.

She only managed to get a few words with Dad, as he was on the point of leaving.

'About Effie, Clare. I haven't forgotten, but I haven't found anything that's been written about her yet. I'm still looking, though.'

'Thanks, Dad.'

Dad gave her a hug, while Vanessa was thanking Mother for the tea. 'See you tomorrow, then. It's good to find you looking so bright. Look after Mother. And don't do anything I wouldn't do.'

She saw him get into Vanessa's car and drive away.

CHAPTER 10

Clare found she was looking forward to meeting Olwen Hughes – the only other person, so far as she knew, who had an obsession with Effie. Obsession was what Jamie called it, and Mother, though she was tolerant enough, clearly didn't understand why Clare needed to find out more and more about her. As for other people, they'd probably think she was mad, if they knew.

Dad called in the afternoon to pick up Jamie, closely shadowed by Vanessa who was wearing another glamorous dress. Clare was glad when they'd gone. It was not that she didn't want to see Dad, but seeing him and Mother in the same room, making polite conversation, had upset her yesterday and it upset her now. Punctually at two there was a knock on the door and Mother let in Olwen. She was quite young, and plump, with dark curly hair. She wore a bright patchwork jacket and slacks, glasses on a cord and carried a huge handbag.

The first thing she said was that she was thrilled to meet some of Effie's family.

'Effie was Mum's great-aunt,' Clare explained, 'so I'm her great-great-niece.'

'But we don't know much about her,' Mother said, 'because my side of the family has never taken an interest in art. Except Clare.'

They took Olwen to see the two oil paintings, the

girl holding the cat and the view of Effie's room in Paris. She looked as if she was about to burst into tears.

'I'd never heard about these two. You see, I've only been working on Effie for a year, and I keep finding new treasures. These are marvellous.'

'How did you get interested in her?' Mother asked.

'Well, I did a degree in art history – I graduated but haven't found a job yet – and someone suggested a project on Cornelius Price and his circle. At that time Effie was just a name to me.'

She was still staring at Effie's pale carnations, as if she couldn't get enough of them.

'But I soon found she was in a different class from the rest. Even Cornelius said she was better than him, and he was a vain old man.'

'He was.' Mother led them back into the sitting-room and arranged chairs. 'Tell me, is it true that Cornelius is getting less popular?'

'Oh, yes.' Olwen blinked seriously through her granny-glasses. 'His star is going down as Effie's rises. Nowadays people think he was quite an ordinary painter who became famous because he went everywhere and knew everyone. But Effie – she was something else. I should hang on to those pictures, Mrs Drummond; they may be worth a fortune one day.'

Clare spread the drawings on the table and Olwen brooded over them like a mother duck.

'But I don't understand,' she said, when she

thought it had gone on long enough. 'I always got the idea that Effie was completely forgotten.'

'Oh, no. No, she was never forgotten. There was a memorial exhibition in London the year after the war. And various galleries have got her work. I'll show you my photos.'

She pulled a bulging envelope out of her bag.

'Five of them are in Paris, and three in the States, and Ruby has two, and Cornelius's grandchildren have some others. I've been travelling round looking at them.'

'This is how you spend your holidays from the bakery?' Mother asked.

'Yes.'

There were over twenty photographs and postcards. The colours made little pools of light on the mahogany table, deep colours like purple, gold, mulberry. They were mostly portraits of women or girls. Sometimes there was a window or curtain in the background, sometimes a book or a desk.

Clare drew a deep breath.

'Yes. They're wonderful.'

'I'll leave you to talk,' Mother said, and went out, first giving them a tray with a pot of coffee and some slices of yesterday's cake.

Olwen said, 'Someone is writing a book about her. And there's a man in France trying to make a complete list of her work. And there are little bits on her in all the books about women artists.'

'My brother says there aren't any women artists.'

'There always have been. Very good, some of them.'

'I'd like to be an artist myself,' Clare said.

'Why shouldn't you?'

They drank coffee and nibbled orange cake in a friendly silence.

'Olwen, do you really think Effie's paintings are valuable?'

'Not yet,' Olwen said, 'but they will be some day.'

'But Effie was quite poor. She starved herself to feed her cats.'

'Yes.'

'Do you think she ever wanted to get married?'

'I think so, but the man was a bastard. He was mixed up with lots of other women – one of them was a sculptress, who went mad. So after he died she put all her energy into her painting.'

Olwen was still staring at Effie's carnations, which had been taken down and propped against the wall. 'I'll give you some advice, Clare. When you go home – you are going, aren't you?'

'Probably.'

'Well, when the time comes you should store these pictures in the bank, because they're too important to keep in an empty house.'

'Right. I'll tell Mum.'

Later Olwen took photographs of the paintings and drawings to add to her collection. She also took Clare's address in Milton Keynes.

'Would you like to have one of the drawings?' Clare asked. 'Only,' – she added quickly – 'not the nice one of the little girl.'

She looked at Mother to see if she objected, but she was smiling.

'Of course take one.'

'Are you *quite* sure?' Olwen asked, and when she was urged, chose a pencil drawing of the cat and carefully packed it away.

'Clare likes cats too,' Mother said, 'so you can see that there's a blood relationship.'

After Olwen had left to catch the Cardiff train they waited for another three hours before Jamie came home. He was by himself and looked flushed and tired.

'Isn't your father coming in?' Mother asked.

Jamie said shortly, 'No.'

'What did you do?'

'Oh, we saw a film, and walked round the shops a bit, and then they took me out to dinner. It was quite a good meal,' he added less gloomily, 'steak, and prawn cocktails, and Black Forest gâteau. I drank half a bottle of wine.'

'Ridiculous,' Mother said. 'Well, you must have an early night . . .'

Suddenly the standard lamp went off. Looking out of the window, Clare saw that all the other lights were dead too.

'Help! A power cut.'

It was nearly nine, getting dark for an August evening.

'Have we got candles, Mum?'

'No, we haven't. I never thought of this. Wait a minute, I'll go and ask old Miss Prosser, next door.'

She got the torch they had used for exploring the loft, and went out. Miss Prosser had lived in the next house years ago when Mother was a girl. She would help if she could.

In the half-dark, Persephone sprang up on to Clare's knees. She stroked her.

'Vanessa's a cow,' Jamie said.

He was sitting at the other end of the big room and she could only see his outline.

'What did she do?'

'Oh, she hung around all the time when anyone with any tact would have gone away. She was so gracious, you wouldn't believe. Asked me what I did at school and about my hobbies, as if I was a child. And just when I was going to ask Dad to come in – you never know, Mum might want to see him – she said they were in a hurry and drove off.'

'*I* think she's disgusting,' Clare said.

'Oh, God, Earwig, you're so stupid, you'd say that whatever she was like.' Clare opened her mouth to protest but he went on. 'She doesn't care about us, of course, just wants Dad for herself.'

'Jamie, do you really think they're going to get married?'

'Or live together. The second, probably.'

The tall trees in Clyne Gardens stood out in solid dark blocks against the pearl-coloured sky. Inside the room she could only see the shapes of windows and furniture, and Effie's pale canvas glimmering through the dusk.

'You don't know that. They might not even be

going out together. I mean, she might just have been visiting her sister, and given Dad a lift.'

Jamie swore.

'What's that for?' Clare asked.

'I know they're having an affair.'

'How?'

'I'll tell you.'

Clare kept quiet. Maybe it was the wine he had drunk, but Jamie seemed to be telling her much more than usual.

'You remember when I went to London, the day after my exams, with my friends?'

'Yes.'

'Well, they were mucking about in an arcade, and I suddenly realized we were only a couple of streets away from Dad's bookshop.' Clare was prepared to bet he'd planned this in advance, but she said nothing. 'So I thought I'd go along and see him. I might even have stayed with him for the weekend, if he'd asked.'

His voice came clearly out of the growing darkness. 'Well, I walked there. They were getting ready to close the shop. And Vanessa was all tarted up, in one of those dresses with no shoulders. She told me they were just going out for dinner. So I said I was only passing through, and I talked for about five minutes and then went back to my friends. They hardly noticed I was gone.'

Clare tightened her hands in Persephone's fur.

'What did Dad do?'

'Looked embarrassed. It can't be much fun being

caught in the act at his age. Anyway, don't tell Mum, because even though she says she doesn't mind about Vanessa, she does.'

The door opened. Mother came in carrying a candle and matches.

'Still sitting in the dark? No one seems to know how long this is going on for. We'll go to bed by candle-light as they did in Effie's time.' She put the candlestick on the marble mantelpiece. 'Jamie, are you all right?'

It was odd how she seemed to know these things by instinct. Clare stood up. What was happening to her family?

'I feel sick,' Jamie growled.

'I'm not surprised, after all that wine. Well, I suggest you go to bed while it's still light enough to see. Come on, Clare.'

Lying in bed, with an extra coat on top of her for warmth, Clare tried to still her thoughts by remembering Effie's pictures. She could almost see them in the thick dark, hanging on the walls of an imaginary museum, each of them so beautiful that it lit the gloom like stained glass windows in a cathedral. But even while she was imagining them, she realized that, for the first time in her twelve years of life, she was worried about Jamie.

CHAPTER 11

The next few days passed slowly and unhappily.
Jamie was out until dark, as usual, and Clare and
her mother had plenty to keep them occupied. But
she kept wandering off by herself and thinking –
for her thoughts went round in circles now – that
there must be something she could do to stop
Vanessa.

Suppose Dad moved to Wales. That might mean
they wouldn't have to leave the house, but it
would obviously all be ruined if Vanessa came too.
She had various wild ideas. Perhaps Jamie could
move in with them, and perhaps he'd make himself
so unpleasant that Vanessa would get fed up and
go away. Or if he and she both moved in, they could
stage some big rows which would hopefully frighten
them off. Or they could put a rubber snake in her
bed or some ants or – she almost told Jamie what
she was thinking, but she just knew he'd say she
was stupid. She was getting very tired of hearing
that. Anyway, it probably wouldn't be allowed to
happen; if Dad was infatuated with Vanessa as he
seemed to be, he wouldn't risk letting her and them
stay under the same roof.

As for Mother, she behaved as if nothing was
wrong at all.

One afternoon, a grey misty day, they walked
along the sea front until they came to the war

memorial. Mother said, 'I'll show you my uncle's name.'

They found it quite soon, in the 1939–45 section among all the Griffithses and Joneses and Evanses:

ALAN JAMES PRICE

'Was Jamie called after him?' asked Clare.

'It's a family name. We did think of calling him James Cornelius, but he wouldn't have liked that.'

'I should think not!'

Clare looked at the names, columns and columns of them carved in the white stone, as the seagulls hooted through the mist.

'All the people that were killed! I just can't take it in.'

Mother said, 'No. My parents always told me how lucky I was to have missed the war.' She added rather violently after a moment, 'I wouldn't have let them take Jamie.'

'You might have had to.'

'What shall we do now, Clare?'

'I'm tired,' Clare said, 'let's go home.'

By the time they got there, the mist had cleared and Persephone was dozing on the window seat in a square of late afternoon sun. It occurred to her, as Mother was unpacking the shopping, that this would make a good picture.

She picked up her pencil and a sheet of thick paper and started to draw.

Perhaps because the house was so quiet, she found she was working better than usual and soon had the outline of the little cat. The lines seemed to have fallen into all the right places; there was nothing to rub out. Now the colours. She worked for some time to get the fur exactly the right shade; faint black like Effie's cat instead of deep black like ink. Then the cushion, which was pale yellow.

'I've forgotten the milk again,' Mother said. 'Do you want to come?'

'No,' Clare said without looking up.

She heard her go out. She finished the main picture, then sketched in the tall window and a fold of curtain. Finally she tinted the rest of the paper in the palest yellow she could find so the viewers' eyes would be drawn at once to the dark shape in the centre.

Persephone got up and walked off.

Clare propped her picture on the marble mantelpiece and looked at it. She didn't quite know now how she'd done it; she'd been working as if in a dream. And it was perfect. Of all the hundreds of drawings she'd done in her life, none had been this good.

She almost jumped out of her skin as the door opened and Jamie, looking hot and weary, came in.

'Where's Mum?'

'Gone out,' Clare said abstractedly.

'God, I'm tired!' Jamie collapsed into the nearest chair. 'Get me a drink, Earwig.'

'I won't,' Clare retorted, 'if you call me that.'

'Well, get me one anyway. I'm dying for some lemonade.'

'Oh!' Clare had walked into the kitchen and seen that she'd drunk the last glass herself. 'It's gone.'

'I suppose *you* had it,' Jamie said.

Like all their rows, it started over something quite unimportant.

'The fact is you're stupid, just bone stupid,' Jamie said scathingly.

'I am not!' Clare shrieked back.

'Yes you *are*. Just look at your report, you got bad marks in nearly everything.'

'That's because I was upset about Mum and Dad – '

She couldn't go on; she didn't know how she was going to cope if Jamie was always picking on her. Especially if he was telling the truth, and she really was stupid.

'Well, I was upset, wasn't I?' Jamie said, 'but I still came top of my year. Let's face it, Earwig, you're not exactly clever.'

'I am!' Clare groped round wildly for something to say. 'I'm good at art.'

'Like that thing?' Jamie glanced scornfully at her lovely picture.

'Yes.'

'Well, I don't think it's much good. You haven't even drawn her whiskers. Just because Cornelius was good doesn't mean you will be. And anyway girls can't – '

'Yes, they can! There was Effie, and Dame Laura Knight, and – '

'Children!' Mother came in and dropped her string bag on the kitchen table. 'Can't I leave you alone for five minutes without a screaming row?'

'He started it, Mum!'

'Baby!'

'He did. He said my picture was no good!'

'Baby!' Jamie said again.

'It looks all right to me.' Mother didn't give the picture more than a glance. 'Jamie, I've told you before, until I'm sick of telling you, will you stop picking quarrels with your sister?'

'Oh, yes,' Jamie said, his eyes darkening, 'blame me.'

'I'm not blaming only you. I know that Clare can be very childish. But since you're the elder, I think you should set her a good example.'

Jamie demanded, his voice going up an octave and nearly breaking, 'Why do you always think it's *my* fault?'

'Mum, he started – '

'Be quiet, Clare.'

'I've had as much as I can stand of that stupid little girl. She doesn't act her age. She runs to you and cries and you take her side.' Clare opened her mouth, but Jamie was in such a rage now that she thought she'd better close it again.

'I do everything you ask, I work and work, and she hardly does anything. And still you like her best!'

'Jamie, that isn't true.' Mother was speaking calmly but she had gone rather white. 'I've always loved you both equally.'

'No you don't, you like him best,' Clare muttered.

Jamie shouted, 'I wish you'd never had her! You never cared about me anyway. Or you wouldn't have broken up my home.'

'Jamie – '

'You did. You know you did!'

Clare was staring at the milk carton which was leaking, a white thread of liquid trickling very slowly along the table and onto the floor. She knew she ought to pick it up but she was too shocked to see Jamie's eyes gushing tears. It was she who was supposed to be the cry-baby, not him.

Jamie went on, and now she knew that the argument wasn't to do with her at all. 'Dad didn't want to leave. I asked him and he said so. *You* made him, and I'll never forgive you, and – Oh, damn, you enjoy seeing me cry, don't you?' And, crying quite openly, he fled into his room, and they heard him bolt the door.

Mother tried for some time to persuade him to open it. But Jamie just cursed, and said he was perfectly all right, and he didn't want to be pestered. They could hear him playing his radio very loudly inside.

They ate supper in near-silence. Mother put a tray of soup and sausages outside Jamie's door, telling him it was there, and a few minutes later they heard him take it in. But he refused to let them come near him.

'Well,' Mother said, 'he can't be too bad, if he's still hungry.'

Clare wasn't sure. Jamie was always hungry.

She tried to talk, but Mother only answered briefly. She was looking pale and shocked. Afterwards they hung around, with the house getting darker, but there were no more sounds from Jamie's room.

'Go to bed, Clare. We'll all feel better in the morning.'

Reluctantly, Clare did.

She found it hard to sleep and tossed about restlessly, switching the lamp on once or twice to see if Effie's picture, the one with the carnations, was there still.

Effie. For a few minutes today, she'd thought that she might have some of her talent. She told herself she had to stop worrying about Jamie. In the morning, as Mother said, he'd have calmed down, and they could make friends.

But still she couldn't sleep. She tried to count sheep jumping over a fence, then coloured the sheep pink and yellow and green but she only felt more wakeful. At last she thought, I'll tell myself the story of my family. As if I was writing it down for a stranger. I know much more about it now than I did a few weeks ago.

First there were Cornelius and Effie growing up in this house. Victorian children. And they both became artists; Cornelius was famous and had three wives and lots of girlfriends and Effie had no one, just lived in France like a hermit and painted those wonderful pictures. A corner of the artist's room in Paris. Young woman holding a cat.

But before that, Effie had been a little girl, younger than herself, wearing mourning for her mother. And Archie, the baby, had grown up to become Mr Archibald Price, solicitor, and had two children of his own. A boy and girl.

She tried to imagine them living, and perhaps fighting, in this very house. The girl, Katie, plain and shy, and very much aware that it was her brother Alan who mattered. But then Alan had been killed, and Katie had gone on living here for long empty years keeping house for her father. Clare hated to think about that.

It seemed to be generally agreed that Archie had turned into an awkward old man. He'd have been proud, probably, of having a famous brother like Cornelius, but he wouldn't have thought twice about Effie's paintings although they were hanging on his walls all that time. Or that he had been unfair to his own daughter.

Well, he had died, and Katie, against all expectation, had married Grandfather, who'd been a widower many years older than herself. They'd gone on living in this house and had just the one child, Anne. Incredible to think of Mother being a little girl.

Clare tossed, hearing a distant clock strike midnight. That was really as much as she knew. Mother had grown up and gone to teacher training college in Cardiff and met Dad. They'd got married within six months and everyone had said they were an ideal couple. And now Dad was gone, and she was here again under the same roof with two children. A boy and girl, Jamie and Clare.

The names changed. Price, Llewellyn, Drummond, and if she ever got married herself her children would have still another name. But the family face went on down the generations and so did other things, perhaps, like a talent for drawing. And another fact which didn't change was that the boys counted more than the girls.

It wasn't Dad and Mother's fault. They had never shown a preference for Jamie, but that made no difference. You just knew that girls were less important; it was like that everywhere in the world.

She wasn't sure if she was awake or sleeping. She

thought she was in a dark gallery with famous pictures on the walls, and she had set up her own little easel to copy them. That's what students had done in Effie's day. And somehow she became aware that Effie was standing behind her and looking over her shoulder, though she'd disappear if Clare turned round. She dipped her brushes in the gold and mauve paint and then thought it was no good, because no one would ever want to see her paintings when there were so many others in the gallery.

She said, 'I can't do it,' and heard Effie's quiet voice. 'Yes, you can, Clare.'

'Clare! Clare!'

She woke up and saw light streaming into the room, heard the Saturday morning traffic. Mother was sitting on her bed and shaking her.

'What's the matter?' she said sleepily.

Mother was in her dressing-gown, very white and with tousled hair.

'Jamie's gone.'

CHAPTER 12

Clare sat up. Half her mind was still back in the dream.

'You're panicking, Mum. He's probably only gone out to buy a comic.'

Mother did indeed look panicky but she tried to speak with her usual calm. 'No, he meant to go. He's taken his bag and several of his clothes. I've checked.'

'What about money?' Clare's first thought was that he might have got on the train to go to Dad in England.

'He's only got a pound or two. He was complaining about it yesterday.'

'Has he taken anything from your purse?'

Mother went and looked. 'No.'

By this time Clare was up and they went along the corridor to Jamie's room. He had slept in the bed. Missing were his red shoulder bag, his spare jeans and two good sweaters, his headphones, toothbrush, comb and the book he'd been reading.

Mother explained, 'I heard a door slam early this morning – the front door. It woke me and I went to see if he was all right. I wanted to talk to him. By the time I'd worked out what was going on, he had a good start.'

They went into the kitchen. Jamie had breakfasted off a pint of milk and a cold apple pie; the remains were still on the table. He'd taken several slices of quiche, bananas, a lump of cheese and some packets of juice.

'Enough to keep him going for the day,' Mother said.

'Perhaps he'll come back this evening,' Clare suggested, 'when he's feeling better.'

Mother's mouth tightened. 'I'm not going to sit here and wait for that.'

'Shall we ring Dad?'

'Your father? No, what could he do? I'll tell him tonight if there's no news. Meanwhile I'm going to ring the police.'

They searched the house to see if Jamie had left a note, because, as Clare pointed out, he'd be furious if they called the police for no reason. But there was nothing. Mother sent Clare off to get dressed while she used the telephone. Then she got dressed too. By that time a very big young policeman was pounding on their door.

Mother offered him coffee and said she was sorry to have dragged him out here before she began her story. The young man listened politely, and wrote down what she said in his notebook, but it seemed to Clare that he wasn't worried in the way they were.

'How old is he, ma'am?' he asked after Mother had told him how there'd been a row the previous night, and how he'd taken his things and left early that morning.

'Sixteen in September.'

Clare saw the policeman relax. If it had been a little child, of course they would have looked everywhere, but someone of almost sixteen was as good as grown up.

'And how tall is he? A full man's size?'

'He's five foot nine.'

'Well, ma'am, I don't think the boy could come to much harm in broad daylight. There was a domestic dispute, you say?' His tone implied these things were always happening. 'You'll likely find that he comes home this evening, when his stomach drives him.'

'He's got no money,' Mother said.

'All the more reason why he won't stay away.' He had a soothing voice with a Valleys accent. 'Could he have gone to his father? Or to any of his friends in Swansea?'

'My ex-husband is in England; Jamie hasn't the train fare to get there. And we don't know anyone else here.'

'He might have got to know people,' Clare pointed out, 'when he was going around on his own.'

She didn't believe, as the policeman clearly did, that Jamie would come home when he had worked off his temper. And she was worried because, while other people might think he was almost an adult, to Mother he was still her little boy. Women got terribly upset about their children. Better perhaps to do what Effie had done, and cut yourself off from everybody, but it was a bit late for that.

'Well, ma'am,' the policeman said, getting up, 'I'm sure it'll be all right, but we'll take a photograph of your son just in case.' Mother handed over the one she always carried in her bag, with Clare's. 'And let us know when he comes home, so we can cross him off our list.'

'If he doesn't come home,' Mother said, 'I suppose there are places where young people sleep rough?'

'Well, we do have a homelessness problem, like other cities.'

'And a drugs problem?'

'Yes, there are young kids with AIDS.' He looked distressed. 'But there's never been anything like that with your boy, has there?'

'No. He was always well-behaved.'

'Then I wouldn't fret.'

The words hung in the air. He was always well-behaved until Dad left home. As they heard the door close behind the policeman Mother said briskly, 'Now Clare, eat your breakfast. We're going to look for him.'

'How can we? He could be anywhere.'

'We'll look in the places where he usually goes.'

Clare swallowed her cornflakes at top speed, and they went out. It was still only five to nine, and as they went down the lane and on to the sunny coast road the noise of traffic assaulted them. The city was on the move.

Jamie would obviously have caught a bus into Swansea. They got on the next that came along, and Clare insisted they should go first to the railway station. Her own strong feeling was that Jamie would try to get to Dad somehow, and he might have a secret store of money. But when they'd got there, and walked around for a while, it became obvious they were wasting their time. There were crowds of people pouring in and out; they had no chance of spotting one boy. After that they looked round the shopping centre and the waterfront, which Jamie loved. There were plenty of people sitting at tables in the open air, breakfasting on coffee and croissants and orange juice, but no sign of him. Then they walked through the bus station; nothing. They didn't bother looking in the museum or art gallery.

Crowds everywhere. People in summer clothes, people talking strange languages, people giving out leaflets. Clare kept thinking that one of the boys in the vast shifting throng looked like Jamie, but it always turned out to be somebody else. Anyway, would it help if they did meet him, she wondered. He might only run away.

After they'd been looking for about two hours, the sun was high in the sky and they were very tired. Mother bought a strong coffee for herself and a glass of milk for Clare. They went in all the shops where Jamie was at all likely to be, scanning the crowds everywhere for his red bag and black anorak. Clare's feet were aching badly now.

At one o'clock they took the bus home and had some bread and salad. Mother also made a meal for Jamie, leaving it prominently on the table.

'Can't I stay here?' Clare begged. 'Then I could answer the phone.'

Besides, she had a feeling that however long they looked, it would be no good.

'No,' Mother said decisively. 'I'm not leaving you too, Clare. Just have a short rest and we'll go.'

They walked to Singleton Park, where Jamie had often gone, and wandered round looking at the people playing tennis. Then back to town, looking into arcades where teenagers crouched over machines and into more and more shops. Clare noticed as they got away from the tourist area how the streets were growing shabbier, bulging bin liners on the pavements and buildings covered with graffiti. A lot of broken windows, too. The city had its underside which she hadn't seen.

In the end she got so tired that she pleaded to be taken home. Mother said, 'I'm sorry, Clare.'

It was late afternoon now, the sun still blazing. They waited a long time for a bus and then wearily walked back up the path of Effie's house. Clare saw Mother tense as they unlocked the door but as soon as they saw the untouched meal on the kitchen table they knew Jamie hadn't come back. She lay down on the ancient sofa and kicked off her shoes.

She was exhausted, and beginning to be very frightened.

'Mother!'

'Yes, Clare?'

Mother came and sat on the sofa next to her, putting her head on her lap.

'Why do you think he ran away?'

Mother's answer was almost inaudible. 'I think Jamie's cracking up.'

'Because I quarrelled with him? Was it something I did?'

Mother said after a moment, 'No, your father and I did it. We were so busy fighting that we never thought what it was doing to you children. Jamie's temper – you doing badly at school – it was all connected.'

'Mum, *couldn't* you ring Dad? Please!'

'I will if he's not home before dark.'

They went on holding each other tightly for the next few minutes. But Clare was getting more and more terrified, as she pictured to herself what might happen to Jamie if he didn't come home. She'd seen programmes about teenagers who drifted to the big cities because they had been thrown out or couldn't get on with their parents. Jamie could be out on the streets of London, as she still half-thought, or somewhere in the drab part of Swansea, who knew? Out there where the kids slept in cardboard boxes or clustered beneath the dirty arches for shelter, sharing needles and passing round the AIDS virus and getting ripped off by any sick or violent stranger who pretended to offer them help. She wondered if that was a roll of thunder she heard in the distance, or was it only traffic? Whether it was going to rain on Jamie tonight.

Mother said, 'You see – they won't believe that he isn't old enough to know what he's doing.

There are lots of boy soldiers in other countries no older than Jamie.'

Clare shut her eyes tightly. She saw the photograph of a young man in khaki, Effie's nephew who had been killed, and he had Jamie's face.

The telephone rang.

CHAPTER 13

Tom Drummond sat behind his desk on the same hot August Saturday, glancing at the clock from time to time. Two more hours, and then he could decently lock up the bookshop and go home along the crowded M1 to the house in Milton Keynes where he lived alone now. After three weeks of his housekeeping, it looked like a tip.

Vanessa was talking.

'So I thought, Tom, there's this dear little Greek restaurant where we could eat, and afterwards we'll go back to my place for a nightcap – '

He'd got a headache.

'That's a nice idea, Vanessa, but I really should go home.'

'Oh, why?' Vanessa said reproachfully.

He was saved from answering because a customer came up to ask her a question. It was very hot, indoors and out. What was he doing here, while his wife, Clare and Jamie were two hundred miles away? He was about to make an excuse and slip out when the telephone rang.

'Mr Drummond?' a man's voice asked. 'Mr Tom Drummond?'

'Yes,'

'This is Euston Road police station. Have you got a son called Jamie?'

When the telephone rang in the house at Black Pill,

Mother seized it. Clare had just time to think that it might be nothing important when she said, '*Tom* – but where?'

Her father's voice, quite strong over the great distance.

'Don't worry. He's with me. That is, we're at home and he's upstairs in the shower – he was filthy. I did try to ring you earlier, but there was no reply. So I left Vanessa to close the shop and brought him home.'

Mother said, 'What happened?'

'Well, I gather he caught the train from Swansea to London this morning. He said he was unhappy there and was coming to me.'

So her hunch had been right, and he'd been in the station at the same time as they were looking for him. Dad went on, 'He hadn't got the fare. So he spent the entire journey dodging the ticket collector – moving from coach to coach, locking himself in the lavatory and so on. Until at last he panicked, and hid under a seat. I told you he was filthy. They caught him and handed him over to the railway police.'

Mother was openly weeping. 'Tom, how is he?'

'Don't cry. He's perfectly safe now. The police rang me and I came round and bailed him out. Luckily the car's repaired, so I drove him straight home. He seemed to relax as soon as I came in. Went to sleep lying on the back seat, poor little chap.'

Mother said, 'I'm so glad, so relieved.' Clare

noticed her small form shaking. A moment later she thought she heard her father say:

'Anne, this has gone on too long.'

But she didn't hear the rest of it, because she suddenly realized she was about to cry too, and it seemed best to rush for the bathroom and lock herself in until she felt human again.

THE END

On Sunday Clare woke late.

Mother had told her Dad was bringing Jamie home, and they might arrive before midnight, but although she'd tried to stay awake she obviously hadn't heard them come in. Heavens, it was half past nine! She'd slept around the clock.

Outside, bells were chiming. The room was full of light and the girl in Effie's picture looked down at her with a calm face.

She got up and looked out of the window. The old car was standing there, so they were obviously here. She looked first in Jamie's room. A lump under the duvet told her that he was fast asleep, Persephone curled up by his feet.

She went downstairs and into the kitchen. Mother and Dad were sitting on different sides of the table with a yellow coffee pot between them. Something in the atmosphere told Clare that she could join them, that they weren't having a row.

'Hello.'

'Hello, monster,' Dad said.

Clare sat down at the table and helped herself to yogurt.

'Is Jamie all right?'

'Yes,' Mother said, 'but we're going to let him sleep as long as he needs. Don't say anything to him about what happened, Clare. He's had a bad time.'

'And how are you, Clare?' Dad enquired.

'Fine. I've been liking it very much in Swansea.'

'That's good, because I've got news. I've been offered the job at the Student Bookshop. So I can move here almost straight away.'

Clare stared at him, not daring to ask questions.

'So how would you like it if we sold the house in Milton Keynes, and came to live in this one?'

'All of us?'

'Yes.'

Clare looked from one to the other of her parents. They seemed serious.

'He means,' said Mother, 'that we're not going to get divorced.'

'But what about Vanessa?' Clare stammered.

Her father looked embarrassed.

'Vanessa was never my girlfriend. We thought of it, but – well, it wouldn't have been a good idea. All I did was take her out a few times, and then when I was coming to Wales she offered me a lift – '

'It's all right, Tom,' her mother said. 'I never believed it was anything serious. I think Jamie did.'

'What annoyed me,' Dad said rather heatedly, 'was that the wretched girl wouldn't leave me alone for a moment and she'd fixed for me to stay at her sister's so I couldn't get out of it. I wanted to spend more time with you and the children.'

'Well, Dad,' Clare said, 'I think you should have told her to go away.'

'I'm afraid your father isn't good at being rude to people,' Mother said.

Clare looked to see if she meant it. She was smiling, and, at long last, she began to believe that things were getting back to normal again. Vanessa would hang around a man for ever, even when it was obvious that he wasn't interested, but Mother would prefer to walk away. Perhaps she was like Effie, determined to do things by herself. Perhaps if she hadn't been, they could have avoided a lot of pain.

'Why did you think about getting divorced?' she asked after a moment.

'That's a hard question,' Dad said.

Mother said, 'We worried about the wrong things. Work, and money. But it's going to be different from now on.'

'I certainly hope so,' Dad said buoyantly. 'We'll move here, and find schools for you both, and – do you want to go to art classes, Clare?'

Art classes! Like Effie.

'I'm not sure if I'm any good, Dad . . .' she began cautiously.

'From the pictures you left around the house, I'd say you were good all right. Why? Has Jamie been telling you that girls can't paint?'

He began to feel in his pocket, but Clare had suddenly remembered something.

'Dad, there's one thing you don't know! Jamie refuses to live here. He made an awful scene when Mum suggested it.'

'I wouldn't worry about that,' Mother said. 'Jamie will be happy enough if his father is here.'

'Are you talking about me?'

Jamie was standing in the doorway, in his pyjamas and bare feet and clutching Persephone. He looked terribly thin, Clare thought, and not properly awake.

'We're just making plans for the future,' Dad said.

Jamie stared at them over the cat's head.

'But you do mean it? You're not going away? I couldn't go through all that again.'

'No,' Mother said very definitely, 'you won't have to. I think we've all been through enough in the last year, and it's time to stop.'

'Wrap yourself up, Jamie,' Dad said, 'and then we'll talk. Clare, I've got you a present.' He brought out a small parcel wrapped in pink paper. 'Why don't you go back to bed and open it?'

Clare went willingly enough. Let them talk to Jamie. She climbed into bed again and unwrapped her parcel. It was a small paperback book with a familiar picture on the front and beneath it the title:
EUPHEMIA PRICE

She flicked through it. It was by an American living in France, who was obviously mad about her, and there were a few pages about Effie's life and then twenty pictures in colour. Marvellous pictures of the subjects Effie had liked best, of women in dark brown or mauve or crimson dresses, of a teapot and a few flowers in a glass jar. But not the two hanging on Clare's wall. She'd have to write to this person; she'd be excited to know there were others.

It would be a long time before she could take them all in. She turned to the introduction and a few words caught her eye:

'Cornelius was one of the most famous painters of his time, while Effie lived and died in obscurity, yet he once said, "A hundred years from now, I shall be remembered mainly as the brother of Euphemia Price".'

Clare read it carefully. He hadn't just said it to be polite, she was sure. The old man might not have been a great genius himself but he'd recognized genius when he saw it. Effie's pictures, mouldering in attics, ignored by the critics who thought a woman couldn't paint. And now they were coming out into the light after fifty years.

She started to get dressed. There was a lot to do. They'd have to go back to England one more time, pack their things and move here, and she would write some letters to various people about Effie, and there would be art classes . . .

Perhaps, she thought, when Jamie's a distinguished old man, he'll say, 'A hundred years from now, I shall be remembered mainly as the brother of Clare Drummond.'

It didn't sound very likely.

But she thought that she and Jamie could probably be friends one day.

POSTSCRIPT

Effie and Cornelius were not real people, any more than Clare and Jamie. But they were suggested by Gwen John and her brother Augustus, who was a famous British painter of the early twentieth century. Gwen lived in Paris, died before Augustus, and was overshadowed by him for many years. But she is now thought to be one of the very greatest modern painters. Her works hang in the Tate Gallery, the National Museum of Wales, the National Gallery of Scotland and many other places in Britain and abroad.

THE AUTHOR

Merryn Williams grew up in the Black Mountains around Hay-on-Wye. She was educated at Cambridge and went on to teach adults for a living. She now lives quietly in Bedfordshire with her husband, two children and a cat, and what is probably the world's largest collection of postcards by women artists. This is her first novel for children.